PUFFIN BOOKS
SECOND THINKS

Maths and science have never been such fun! In the hands of Johnny Ball, all sorts of scientific and mathematical principles suddenly come to life in the most entertaining way. Mirrors, mazes, cards, codes, paper, string, balance – puzzles, tricks and projects featuring all these, and more, lie in wait. In Johnny Ball's inimitable style, even the most complex-sounding facts are explained in a way that's clear, interesting and often hilarious! This is an entertaining and fascinating book that not only will make you think but will also give you hours of fun and a lot of laughs!

Johnny Ball started working life as a comic on the northern club circuit. He first appeared on TV in the children's musical shows *Playschool* and *Playaway* and was then given his own series on science and maths subjects, including the very successful *Think of a Number*. He is one of today's most popular children's television personalities. Johnny Ball lives in Berkshire with his wife and family.

# Johnny Ball's
# SECOND THINKS

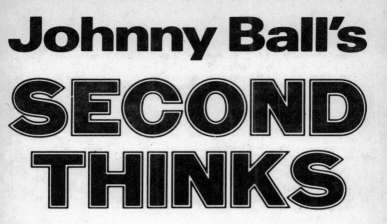

## Illustrated by
## David Woodroffe

PUFFIN BOOKS

Puffin Books, Penguin Books Ltd, Harmondsworth, Middlesex, England
Viking Penguin Inc., 40 West 23rd Street, New York, New York 10010, U.S.A.
Penguin Books Australia Ltd, Ringwood, Victoria, Australia
Penguin Books Canada Ltd, 2801 John Street, Markham, Ontario, Canada L3R1B4
Penguin Books (N.Z.) Ltd, 182–190 Wairau Road, Auckland 10, New Zealand

First published 1987

Made and printed in Great Britain by
Cox & Wyman Ltd, Reading, Berks.
Typeset in Linotron Baskerville by
Rowland Phototypesetting Ltd
Bury St Edmunds, Suffolk

# Contents

I only needed to think for a second before dedicating *Second Thinks* to my own children, Danny, Nicky and Zoë.

# Introduction

Hello there!

When I'm writing any one of the 'Think of a Number', 'Think Again' or 'Think It – Do It' programmes for BBC Television, or a 'Johnny Ball Maths Games' for radio, I always try to pack in as many ideas as will possibly fit into the allotted time. Similarly with this book, I've tried to squeeze as much as I possibly could into 175 pages.

In the book, as you meander through mazes (Chapter 1), deal with cards (Chapter 2), reflect on mirror images (Chapter 3), get wrapped up in paper planes (Chapter 4) or tied in knots (Chapter 5), I hope you keep your balance (Chapter 6) and patience (Chapter 7) until the very end, when you should be left with no illusions (Chapter 8), other than that things mathematical and scientific can be great fun once you have found the way to break the code of mystery (Chapter 9) which surrounds them – and I'm sure you will find that they're not just for squares (Chapter 10)!

Best wishes.

Cheers,

# CHAPTER 1

# The Maze of Ways from A to B

Writing a book is rather like going on a long journey. You know where you are (at the beginning) and you know where you want to get to (the end). The big problem is, what route should you take? I'm sure you know that the shortest distance between two points is a straight line, but if you decide now to go somewhere in a straight line, after going just a few paces you will probably come to a sudden stop and say, 'Ouch!' If the pain is in your leg, you will have walked into the furniture, but if the pain is in your nose, you will have walked into the wall. And it's no good me telling you to stop being stupid and sit down – with your nose right up against the wall, you won't be able to read this book.

## Map Meddling

A few years ago, my wife and I drove to Penzance, where I had been asked to give a lecture. The journey took seven hours – five hours of driving and two hours to refold the maps. Now why is it so difficult to refold unfolded folding maps? It's because there are an enormous number of ways to do it.

Even a simple eight-sheet map can be folded forty

different ways, all with the same corner section upper-most. Try it and see. Or try these!

Take four sheets of paper and fold them in half three times, so that they form eight sections in two rows of four. Then number the sections as shown in the illustrations. You will need to number each section on both sides, making sure that it has the same number on the back and the front. The object is to fold each sheet so that the sections are in numerical order, with 1 showing on the top and 8 on the bottom. Have a go and try it out on your friends. It starts off easy, but gets more and more difficult. If you get really stuck, you'll find the solutions at the end of this chapter.

# Follow That Cab!

Have you ever wondered why country roads are often so twisty and winding? My theory is that in the old days people weren't very good at measuring long distances and, when they were building a road, they were always worried that it might end up too short. So, to be on the safe side, they always built their roads longer than they needed to. However, because they made them too long, they had to bend the roads quite a lot to fit them in between the villages.

What do you mean 'Rubbish'?

Anyway, I'm sure most people prefer winding country roads to monotonous, straight, parallel city streets that criss-cross each other at right angles, like those in New York or in our illustration below.

New York's street layout may be efficient, but, as any New York taxi-driver knows, there's no such thing as a

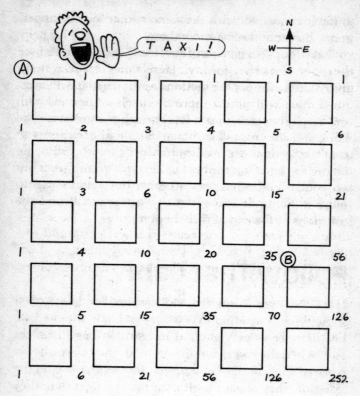

short cut. Say you want to get from point A to point B; you could go east for four blocks and then south for three blocks, making a journey of seven blocks. Or, if you liked, you could zigzag – east for one block and then south for one block and so on – but you would still have to travel seven blocks to get to B: four along and three down. The question is, how many different seven-block routes could you take to get from A to B? Well, there are several ways to work it out. One is by tracing all the possible routes between A and B, and keeping count of them. But here's an ingenious way which will also help you work out the number of routes between A and *any* of the other blocks in the 'city'. Here's how it works: first, give each of the road junctions a number, as we have done. Starting from A, there is only one direct way to reach any junction on the top line – by going east – so we have put a 1 at each junction. Similarly, there is only one direct way to any of the junctions directly south, so they also have a number 1. To reach the junction south-east of A, there are two possible routes – south then east, or east then south – so we have put a 2 at that junction, and so on. Each new number is found by adding together the number to the north of it and the number to the west of it. Using this system, we find that there are thirty-five different seven-block routes between A and B.

The numbers can be written out in triangular formation; the pattern they make is known as 'Pascal's Triangle'. 'Pascal's Triangle' has lots of

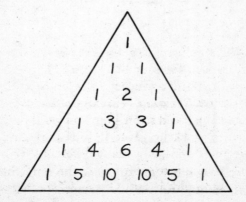

amazing properties which I won't go into now, but it can also be used to perform a very good card trick. Read on!

# The Great Pyramid Trick

Take a pack of cards and remove all the Tens and picture cards, leaving the thirty-six cards from Ace (or One) to Nine. Ask someone to make up the first row of the pyramid by dealing out four cards, face up. When he's done this, take the rest of the pack back, and secretly select a card which you place face down, as shown in the illustration.

| 1 | 6 | 4 | 2 |

Then tell your helper to follow the following rules which you want him to follow . . . are you following all this? Ask him to form the second row of the pyramid by adding together the face value of the first and second cards in the first row (in our example we would get 1 + 6 = 7). He picks a card showing a Seven out of the pack and places it above the Ace and the Six. Next, your helper adds together the second and third cards in the first row (6 + 4 = 10). If, as in this case, the answer is a two-digit number, he must add the two digits together to get a one-digit number: 1 + 0 = 1. So an Ace is placed above the Six and the Four. Then the third and fourth cards in the first row must be added together (4 + 2 = 6) and a Six completes the second row of the pyramid.

Following the same pattern, an Eight and a Seven form the third row of the pyramid (7 + 1 = 8 and 1 + 6 = 7). Now, by adding those two cards together, we get 8 + 7 = 15, and, reducing that to a single digit, we get 1 + 5 = 6. On turning over the top card, we find it is . . . a Six! Amazing.

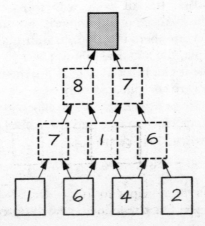

The trick always works and the only difficult bit is working out just which card to place face down at the top when you begin the trick. To do that, go back to Pascal's Triangle and look at the third row: it contains the numbers 1, 3, 3 and 1 – OK? So, in our trick, when the first four cards are dealt, we must do a bit of mental arithmetic: multiply the middle two cards by 3 and then add the result to the two outside cards (in our example, $6 + 4 = 10 \times 3 = 30 + 1 + 2 = 33$). Reduce that to a single digit ($3 + 3 = 6$) and you know that the top card which you place face down at the start of the trick has to be a 'Six'. With a little practice, it's easy.

# Here Lies John Rennie

Let's go back to our New York taxi ride. Remember I told you there were several ways of working out how many routes there were between points A and B? Well here's another. It's all to do with things called factorials. (The factorial of a number is that number and all the other numbers less than it multiplied together – for example, the factorial of 3 is $3 \times 2 \times 1 = 6$.) To explain how it can be used here, I'll write down what looks like a very complicated sum.

The trip from A to B is a seven-block journey, and point B is four blocks along and three blocks down; so the sum is written out like this:

$$\frac{7 \times 6 \times 5 \times 4 \times 3 \times 2 \times 1}{4 \times 3 \times 2 \times 1 \ \times \ 3 \times 2 \times 1}$$

Now we cancel out above and below the line:

$$\frac{7 \times \cancel{6} \times 5 \times \cancel{4} \times \cancel{3} \times \cancel{2} \times \cancel{1}}{\cancel{4} \times \cancel{3} \times \cancel{2} \times \cancel{1} \times \cancel{3} \times \cancel{2} \times 1}$$

leaving:

$$\frac{7 \times 5}{1} = 35 \text{ different routes.}$$

You really need to remember this method if you want to solve the problem of the 'Monmouth Tombstone'.

The Monmouth Tombstone is to be found in a graveyard in Monmouth, South Wales. The tombstone is dedicated to John Rennie, and he must have been some kind of joker, because the tombstone is covered in letters. Reading from the centre and zigzagging in any direction towards one of the four corners, the letters always spell out 'Here lies John Rennie', no matter how long or how short any of the zigzags are. Can you work out how many different versions of the sentence there are on this tombstone? Well, using factorials makes it easy . . . Just in case you get stuck, the answer is at the end of the chapter.

# Amazing Mazes

We can't talk about the maze of ways from A to B without talking about mazes themselves, and the most amazing thing about mazes is that there isn't always a maze of ways through them – there is usually only one.

This is the most common, simple maze design, which has been found all over the world:

It has cropped up in England, Finland, India, Peru, North America and many Mediterranean countries.

No one knows how this design travelled or where it was first invented, although the earliest record of it is thought to be one found on a 2,500-year-old Italian vase – there was a picture on it that looked a bit like this:

What we do know, however, is that it's very easy to learn to draw it.

The Christian Church teaches that the path to Heaven is not straight and even, but long and difficult, and this may be the reason why very elaborate mazes can be found on the floors of many churches and cathedrals (like the one below from Ely Cathedral). Perhaps worshippers would meander round them while praying – they may even have gone round on their knees?

And what about mazes that you can actually get lost in, like the one at Hampton Court, built in 1690, or the

modern one at Blackpool Pleasurebeach? Now it's very hard to find your way out of these mazes if you're in them, surrounded by tall hedges, but it's a lot easier to find your way round a *map* of a maze. However, here is a map of a different kind of maze, which you may find quite difficult. The idea is to start at 'S' and finish at 'F', visiting as many squares as you like, but none twice. As you go along, add up the numbers in the squares you pass through. The object is to make the highest score (it's more than 280). Good luck.

| S | 4 | 2 |   | F | 9 | 9 | 6 | 3 | 2 | 4 |
|---|---|---|---|---|---|---|---|---|---|---|
| 2 |   | 3 |   | 3 |   | 1 |   | 8 |   | 2 |
| 8 | 4 | 0 | 7 | 1 | 2 | 3 | 6 | 9 | 0 | 1 |
|   | 6 |   | 4 |   | 8 |   |   | 2 |   |   |
|   | 8 |   | 9 | 4 | 6 | 5 | 9 | 7 | 2 | 6 |
| 2 | 7 | 9 |   | 2 |   | 0 |   | 9 |   | 1 |
| 6 |   | 8 | 2 | 7 |   | 3 |   | 6 | 1 | 0 |
| 7 | 9 | 5 |   | 3 | 1 | 8 | 7 | 2 |   | 4 |
| 3 |   | 2 | 7 | 1 |   | 6 |   | 5 | 5 | 1 |
| 2 |   | 0 |   | 0 | 2 | 1 |   | 8 |   | 0 |
| 0 | 1 | 2 | 3 | 1 |   | 2 | 3 | 1 | 0 | 3 |

# The Labyrinth

The most famous of all mazes is the legendary Cretan Labyrinth that was inhabited by the Minotaur, a monster half-man and half-bull. The story goes that Theseus entered the Labyrinth and killed the Minotaur. He managed to get out of the Labyrinth again by following a silk thread (given to him by Ariadne, King Minos' daughter) which he had trailed behind him. The thread idea had come from Daedalus, the architect of the Labyrinth. When King Minos found out, he had Daedalus thrown into the Labyrinth without a thread. Daedalus found it impossible to get out of the Labyrinth, even though he had built it in the first place. Of course, the story is only a legend, but perhaps it was inspired by the real-life labyrinth built 4,000 years ago for the Egyptian Pharaoh, Amenemhet III. This building was two storeys high and totally without windows. It measured 250 metres along each side and contained 3,000 rooms!

# Answers

## Map Meddling

**1238**
**6547**
Fold 2 and 5 over on to 3 and 4.
Fold 1 and 6 left on to 2 and 5.
Fold 6 and 7 up behind 1 and 8.
Fold 8 behind 1.


**1456**
**2387**
Fold 6 and 7 behind 5 and 8.
Fold 2, 3 and 8 up behind 1, 4 and 5.
Fold 5 on to 4.
Fold 8 behind 1.


**1874**
**2365**
Fold the sheet in half, bringing 4 behind 1.
Fold 2 and 3 up behind 1 and 8.
Find 4 and 5 inside, and tuck them between 3 and 6.
Fold 8 behind 1.

**1827**

**4536**

Fold the bottom half up behind the top half.

Take 7 back and round in a loop.

Thread 7 between 1 and 4. Keep threading until 7 is behind 8.

Square up the packet and, peeping between the sheets, you'll see that they are in order. And what's more, they won't unfold easily.

# Here Lies John Rennie

The tombstone problem is solved by calculating the number of routes to any one corner of the tombstone and then multiplying by 4. Let's take the bottom right-hand corner. Starting at the central 'H', each route is 17 steps long, 8 across and 9 down. So, using factorials, the sum you need to work out is:

$$\frac{17 \times 16 \times 15 \times 14 \times 13 \times 12 \times 11 \times 10 \times 9 \times 8 \times 7 \times 6 \times 5 \times 4 \times 3 \times 2 \times 1}{9 \times 8 \times 7 \times 6 \times 5 \times 4 \times 3 \times 2 \times 1 \quad \times \quad 8 \times 7 \times 6 \times 5 \times 4 \times 3 \times 2 \times 1}$$

When you cancel out above and below the line, you get the answer 24,310 which needs to be multiplied by 4 for the four corners, so 24,310 × 4 = 97,240 different ways to spell 'Here lies John Rennie'. If poor old John Rennie has to lie so many different ways, he must be constantly turning in his grave. Phew!

# Amazing Mazes

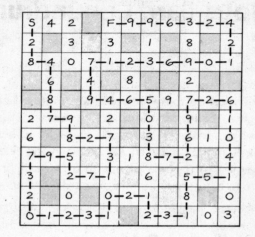

# CHAPTER 2

# Curious Card Conundrums

Why is it that so many people hate maths, but love magic? It's really very strange, because maths and magic make such good partners. To prove it, here are some mathemagical card tricks, and each and every one of them works by itself. Well, not quite by itself, because you have to be there to handle the cards, of course.

## Finger-licking Odd

For this trick you will need another pair of hands, and they mustn't be sticky, so ask your helper to lick her fingers clean – or she could wash them – and then dry them. If there's no towel handy, you can always dry your hands by waving them out of an open window on a sunny day, but don't try this method after having a bath.

Right. Now ask your handy helper to hold her hands out in front of you, palms down. She could even rest them on a table. You then place two cards between the thumb and first finger of her left hand, two cards between the first and second fingers, two cards between the second and third fingers and two cards between the third and fourth fingers. Now for the right hand. Place two cards between the thumb and first finger, two cards

between the first and second fingers, two cards between
the second and third fingers and . . . wait for it . . . only
O N E card between the third and fourth fingers. So far,
so good. Now, starting from your left (her right, right?),
take the first pair of cards, separate them, and place
them on the table. Then take the next two cards,
separate them, and place them on the first two, forming
two piles. Continue, taking each pair and dividing it
into two piles until you come to the last, 'odd' card.

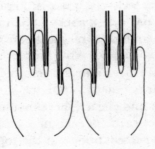

Now ask your helper, 'Which pile shall I put the odd
card on to?' Let's assume she chooses the pile on the
left. You drop the odd card on to the left-hand pile and
say, 'Right. I shall now make the odd card jump from
the left-hand pile to the right-hand pile.' You can add
some magic words, but there is really no need, as the
trick is already done. You pick up the left-hand pile and
show that the cards can be split into pairs without an
odd card being left over. Now ask your helper to
examine the right-hand pile. If she splits it up into
pairs, she will end up with one odd card left, right? How
odd, but how does it work?

Well, you started with seven pairs of cards and one

odd card. Each of your piles contained seven cards, but by adding the odd card to one pile, it would make that pile even, whereas the other pile would still remain odd, oddly enough. Try it and you'll see.

# What's in a Name?

Besides being mind-boggling and baffling, this trick has the added attraction of working if you use your name or my name or anybody else's name. First find a pack of cards and a helper with a name. (You must check your helper's name and be sure you know how he or she spells it.)

Now turn your back and ask your helper to deal out two piles of cards quietly – quietly, so that you can't hear how many and cheat. There should be exactly the same number of cards in each pile, and less than ten. Now ask your helper to look at the top card of those remaining in the pack. He must remember the card, replace it face down, and then put one of his two piles on top of it, also face down. He must hide the other small pile behind his back or in his pocket. You now turn round and pick up the pack of cards, place it behind your back and appear to go into a trance. (This is while you perform your 'magic'.) Secretly, to yourself, you spell out your helper's name and, for each letter, you must deal a card from the top of the pack into your right hand. (If you're not used to handling cards, this will take a bit of practice. You could do it under the table, as long as it's out of sight of your audience.) So, if *I* was helping you, you would spell out JOHNNY BALL and, while doing so, deal ten cards into your right hand, one at a time. This reverses their order; you then place these cards back on top of the pack and put the pack on the table. Now ask your helper to replace the cards he has kept hidden, on top of the pack. Finally, ask him to spell out his name (in this case it would be JOHNNY BALL) and, at the same time, to deal one card face up on to the table for each letter. The mesmerizingly brain-scrambling surprise comes as he deals the last card, because it happens to be the card he looked at while your back was turned.

Try it . . . it works every time. There's only one thing to watch: the name spelt out must contain more letters than there are in each of the original piles.

# Two Wrongs Do Make a Right

Before you perform this trick, you must point out that you have to memorize the entire pack of cards. Take the pack of cards in your right hand and run your left thumb across the top of the cards, making them 'ZIPP' past your thumb, in the same way as you riffle through the pages of a book.

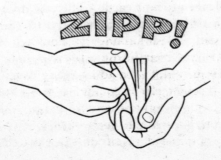

This takes all of two seconds, and you now announce that your lightning brain has remembered the position of every single card. Hand the pack to your helper and ask her to 'think of a number'. (Hey, that's a good name for a television programme . . .) Let's assume she chooses the number 6. Ask her to deal a pile of 6 cards, face down, one at a time, on to the table. Then say, 'Ah, yes . . . I remember . . . the next card will be the Ace of Clubs.' Your helper turns over the next card and is astonished to discover that it isn't the Ace of Clubs . . . Oops!

Ask her to replace the card on the rest of the pack and then place the other 6 cards on top of them. Then ask her to think of a bigger number. We'll assume she now chooses 14. Tell her to repeat the procedure, dealing out a pile of 14 cards, face down, one at a time. Then say, 'Ah, yes, that's it . . . this time the next card is the Ace of Clubs.' She looks at the top card, and this time it still isn't the Ace of Clubs . . . Double oops!

She must replace the card and then place the 14 cards on top. Then you say, 'OK, er . . . let's take one number from the other – that's fourteen minus six, which leaves . . . er . . . um . . . eight.' (It's always good to let your helper have time to do your sum for you.) Now say, 'Right, deal out eight cards.' This she does and then, when you ask her to look at the next card, she'll be quite bamboozled to find that it really *is* the Ace of Clubs!

The magic of this trick happens when you pretend to memorize the cards at the beginning. What you actually do is memorize the top card. In this case, it would have been the Ace of Clubs, and, although you appeared to get the trick wrong twice, really you were just preparing to get it right the third time. Golly gosh.

## The Race to Trace and Displace Every Ace

This is another trick that works mathemagically, but it needs a little preparation. First find the four Aces, place them on top of the pack and then place eight other cards on top of them, so that the Aces take up the positions 9, 10, 11 and 12 in the pack. Now you are ready to go, but don't go till you've done the trick.

Give someone the pack and ask him to think of a number between ten and twenty. Let's say he chooses thirteen. Ask him to deal thirteen cards, one at a time and face down, into a pile on the table. When he's done this, ask him to add together the digits of the number he chose (in this case, 1 + 3 = 4). Then ask him to pick up the thirteen cards and deal four back on to the top of the pack. Now if he turns over the next card in his hand, it will be an Ace. Wow. Ask him to put the Ace to one side, replace the remaining cards on top of the pack and do it all again, choosing a different number between ten and twenty. If he follows the same procedure exactly, no matter what numbers he chooses, after four tries he will have traced and displaced every Ace, and he'll be suitably am-ace-d!

# The Last Card Trick

Actually, this isn't the last card trick. That comes after this trick which, alas, happens to be called the last card trick, because the object is to identify the card which will be dealt last.

Offer someone the pack of cards and ask her to take some cards from the top. She can take a couple or the whole pack – it's up to her. You then take her selected cards, fan them out on the table while they are face down, and then pick out and show just one card to her, without looking at it yourself. 'Remember this card,' you say to your helper, 'as it will cling to your hand until the very last!' You then replace the card in the fan, square up the cards, hand them to her, and ask her to deal them out in this particular way: she must take the top card and place it at the bottom of the pile, then deal the next card face up on to the table. She then places the next card on the bottom of the pile again and deals the following card on to the table. She must continue to do this until she has dealt all the cards out, and, surprise surprise . . . the one you showed her at the beginning of the trick will be the very last card in her hands. But how?

When she hands you the cards she has chosen, you fan them out, counting them as you go and starting from the top. At the same time, you push forward with your left thumb the cards in positions that are powers of two – that means those cards in positions 2, 4, 8, 16

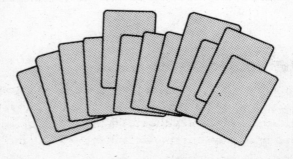

(and, if you have that many, the card in position 32). These are your signpost cards. When you get to the end, you count the number of cards beyond the last signpost card. Then you double that number and add one; the card in that position is the one which you show to your helper.

As an example, if she gives you twelve cards, you push forward with your left thumb cards 2, 4 and 8, and then find there are four more cards after the eighth. $4 \times 2 = 8 + 1 = 9$, so you find the ninth card, which is the one after your signposted eighth card. This you show to your helper and when she deals the cards as per your instructions, the ninth card will always be the last one dealt. The following table shows how to make the trick work for several selected numbers of cards:

| Number of cards chosen | Highest signpost card | $(\times 2 + 1)$ | Position of last card |
|---|---|---|---|
| 6 | 6 − 4 | $= 2 \times 2 = 4 + 1 =$ | 5th |
| 13 | 13 − 8 | $= 5 \times 2 = 10 + 1 =$ | 11th |
| 15 | 15 − 8 | $= 7 \times 2 = 14 + 1 =$ | 15th |
| 16 | 16 − 16 | $= 0 \times 2 = 0 + 1 =$ | 1st |
| 26 | 26 − 16 | $= 10 \times 2 = 20 + 1 =$ | 21st |
| 52 | 52 − 32 | $= 20 \times 2 = 40 + 1 =$ | 41st |

# Look, No Hands

Without question, this is my favourite of all card tricks. I love it because it works mathemagically, without the magician ever touching the cards.

Give your helper the pack of fifty-two cards which he

may shuffle. He then deals nine cards face down on the table, selects just one of them and memorizes it. He then piles up the nine cards, with the memorized card on top, and places the rest of the pack on top of that. You now ask him to start dealing cards, one at a time, face up in a pile on the table. As he does it, he should count backwards from ten – one number for each card dealt. Now, if any card happens to be the same number as the number being called, he must stop there and start a new pile. If no card number is the same as a number called, as soon as he has dealt the tenth card in the pile, he must 'close it' by dealing another card face down on top of that pile.

This he does until he has four piles. In our example, the first two piles of ten were 'closed', as no number

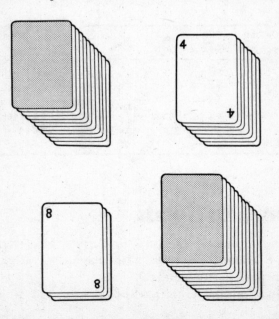

coincided. Of the other two piles, a Four and an Eight were dealt as that number was being called out. Now ask your helper to add together the numbers of the top cards showing – in this case we get $8 + 4 = 12$. From the remaining cards, he must deal out that number (12) face up on to the table. He will be stupefied to see that the card he chose will be the last card dealt.

Even if he tries the whole trick again, he'll be just as mystified as to why and how it works. The secret is that the whole trick is just a devious way of arriving at the card in the 44th position in the pack.

# CHAPTER 3

# The World the Wrong Way Round

What happens when you look into a mirror? You come face to face with the face facing you, and if you manage not to faint with the shock, you may notice that the face you are facing is *your* face. But what else do you notice?

Well, if you wink your left eye, or waggle your left ear, or twitch your left nose, the face facing you seems to wink or waggle or twitch its right eye or ear or nose, which means that all your left bits have somehow become right bits in the mirror. It's enough to make your head itch, and if you scratch the top of your head, the face facing you also scratches the top of its head. But why? If your left bits become your right bits in the mirror, why doesn't your top become your . . . other end? Well, stop scratching (either end) and I'll try to explain, although even the correct explanation often leaves people a little mixed up.

Now, your right and left bits don't actually swap over at all. The reflection of your left ear is still on the left side of the mirror, and the reflection of your right eye is still on the right side of the mirror, just as the top of your head is still at the top and your bottom is . . . where it's always been.

To explain the whole thing better, we really need two mirrors, set at right angles to each other. When I was a lad, my mother had a dressing-table with mirrors on hinges which were perfect for this experiment, but perhaps you can borrow two small mirrors and tape them together (or buy some, they only cost a few pence each in the shops).

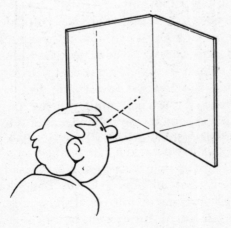

When you look into two mirrors set at right angles to each other, you come face to face with the face other people face when they are facing you. This is the real you, and this time everything has been swapped over from left to right and vice versa. When you wink your left eye, your image's left eye winks too, but you can see that it's on the right side of the mirror. To prove that everything has swapped over, try tilting your head to the side. If you tilt to the left, the image's head tilts to the right – until eventually your head turns completely upside-down.

# Your Two Faces Are Different from One

While you have two mirrors, you can try this experiment and discover that you are actually two-faced.

Move to your left, so that your face is directly facing the mirror on the right, and position the left mirror so that its edge touches your nose. With a little adjustment, you should be able to see a complete face made up of two views of the right side of your face.

Then move to the right until you are facing the left-hand mirror, and the right-hand mirror is touching your nose: you should now see a complete face formed

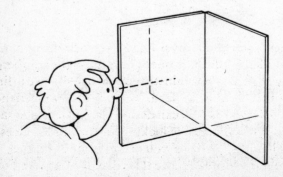

by two views of the left side of your face. Careful examination should show that each side of your face is slightly different.

Usually, the older a person is, the more obvious the difference is, with the left side of the face tending to show a little more strain than the right side over the years.

# Keeping You All on Edge

In the last experiment, the effect of making half a face look like a complete face was achieved using one mirror on its edge. There are lots of things you can do with a mirror on its edge. Forget your own faces for a minute and look at the funny face here. The simple soul on page 43 is just waiting for you to have fun with him. All you need is a small mirror held on its edge (even a shiny box would do)

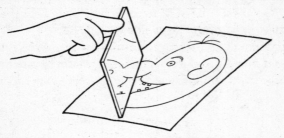

and then you can discover lots of weird and wonderful faces hidden in the main one. There are eight numbered faces on page 42. Try against the clock to see if you can find them all on the 'master' face. Then see how your friends get on. Afterwards, you can design your own master face and set others the task of looking for the hidden faces.

Incidentally, in case you have trouble finding all eight of our weird faces, we'll let you in on a secret: one of them is impossible to find! The question is . . . which one?

# It Comes Right Out at You

While you have a mirror handy, try this next experiment. Over the page are two pictures that look almost alike. However, the right-hand one was drawn from a slightly different angle and the drawing has been reversed. Now hold a small mirror against the right side of your nose and look down at the two pictures. Look straight at the left picture with your left eye and move the mirror about until your right eye can see a reflection

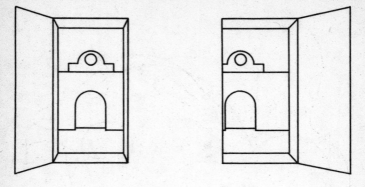

of the right drawing in the mirror. A bit more movement will bring the two images together and you should
see that the background definitely seems further away
than the actual doorway. What you are seeing is a
stereoscopic 3 D effect . . . and all at no extra charge!

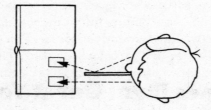

# CRAZY GOLF

Here's a game I used to play at school, using a mirror.
What you see opposite is a map of a golf course. But the
golf course is all in reverse, and you must only look at it
through your mirror standing on its edge. If you think
you might be tempted to cheat, stand a large book up on

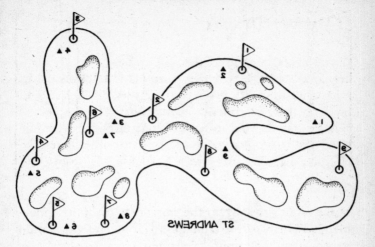

its edge in front of the drawing, so that you can't see it directly. The idea is to trace a path round the course with a pencil, starting at the first 'tee' and tracing a line to the first hole, continuing from the second tee to the second hole, and so on round the course. You may place your pencil on the first tee before you start, but then you should try to draw lines as straight as you can, looking only at the mirror image of the course. You mustn't touch any line on the drawing, so your line will have to have changes of direction in order to avoid the obstacles and reach the holes. Each change of direction counts as one 'stroke'. Any line you hit costs you two strokes, and when you hit a line you must return to the previous tee and start that hole again. Of course this course will only last for a couple of rounds, but once you've got the idea, you can design your own courses for your friends to try, making them harder all the time.

Mirror-writing

If you are any good at the golf game, perhaps you'll be clever enough to write your name backwards, in mirror-writing. What do you think? Well, before you try it, try this experiment *without* a mirror. Find a piece of card or paper, hold it against your forehead with one hand and write your name on it with the other hand. Go on, have a go, because I want you to see the result . . .

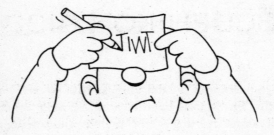

It's amazing, but well over half the people who try this find that they write their own name backwards in mirror-writing, without thinking about it. What happens is that they think of the side of the paper touching their forehead as the front and they imagine the letters appearing on that surface, even though they are writing on the other side. So they write backwards without any effort. Even people who write their names forwards in this experiment find that often some letters are reversed.

O K. Now try writing backwards, using a mirror on its edge. It's quite difficult at first, but with practice it's amazing how quickly your brain gets the hang of it.

Leonardo da Vinci, the famous artist and inventor, wrote everything backwards in mirror-writing. It may have started because he was left-handed, but later on, when he produced so many inventions, it probably came in handy for keeping his notes secret. It was Leonardo's own secret code. The whole of Chapter 10 of this book is about codes, but meanwhile here is a mirror code for you to experiment with. What do all these block capitals and numbers have in common?

-BCDEHIKOX 0138-

Well, if you line up your mirror along the dotted line, you will cut every letter in half – but, thanks to the mirror, you will still see the complete set of letters from either side. They all have horizontal symmetry, and even with as few letters as this, it's surprising how many words you can make up. See if you can decipher these sentences:

DICK HOOKED 1030

CHOICE COD

DEBBIE DICED COD-

COOKED COD

I BOOKED I CHOICE

BOX-CHECKED IN HID

CHOC BOX

HOCKED KIDDIE BIKE

DECIDED IN HIKE

The letters and numbers opposite are also symmetrical, but in a different way. They have vertical symmetry, as you will see if you place your mirror on edge, parallel with the side edge of the book, splitting the letters in the left-hand column down the middle. Can you decipher these coded sentences?

# Calculatingly Clever

If you've got a pocket calculator handy, you don't need a mirror to create a crafty code. No fewer than eight of the calculator digits, when turned upside down, produce quite recognizable letters:

|   |   |   |   |
|---|---|---|---|
| 1: | I I | 6: | 9 |
| 2: | 2 | 7: | L L |
| 3: | E E | 8: | B B |
| 4: | h h | 9: | 6 G |
| 5: | S S | 0: | o o |

So with this information, look at the list of numbers which are all answers to the clues on page 50.

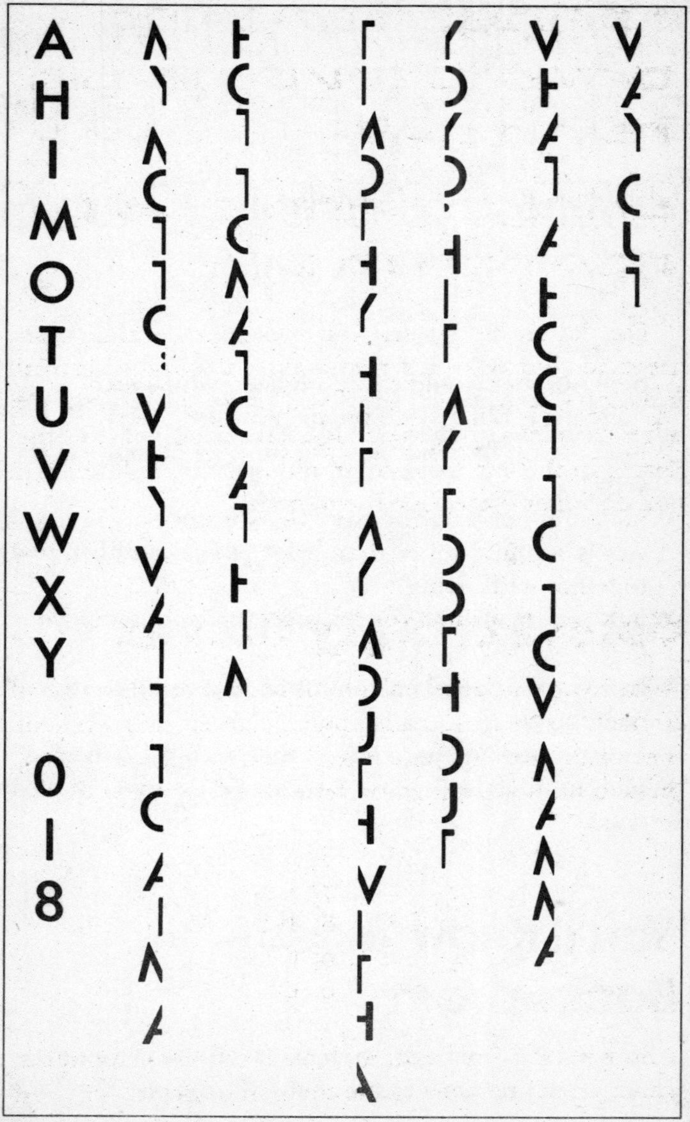

A
H
I
M
O
T
U
V
W
X
Y
O
I
8

7 10 77345     3373 1770

3718804     53704     3 18808

49 1375     378 18     3 179009

3045

Which number would cover a hole in your sock?

Which one is Ollie Lee's phone number?

Which book sells more than this number of copies every year?

Which number is apt to leave you stumped?

A net is nothing more than a lot of this number tied together with string.

What would you do if you dropped this number on your foot?

Which is the telephone number of a multi-national company?

Which number keeps Santa on time with his deliveries?

Which number will get you the same as if you dialled 999?

# You'll Know These Backwards

Any word that spells the same backwards as forwards is called a 'palindrome'. One of the shortest is 'Eve', the first woman, and the first words she ever heard may have been another palindrome: 'Madam, I'm Adam.'

Other palindromes include 'redivider', 'a man, a plan, a canal: Panama', and 'Was it a car or a cat I saw?'

You can make quite long sentences that are palindromes: 'Dennis and Edna sinned' can be extended to make 'Dennis, Nell, Edna, Leon, Noel and Ellen sinned.' Or what about this sentence: '"Evil bats in a cave", sides reversed, is "Eva can I stab live".'

The palindromic record is held by a man in Bewdley, Mr Edward Benbow, who has compiled a composition which doesn't make a great deal of sense, but contains an astonishing 22,500 words.

The reason I've brought all this up is that you can also get palindromic numbers, and making them is incredibly easy. Take any number with more than one digit . . . reverse it . . . add the two numbers together . . . and you'll be surprised how often the result is a palindrome:

$$
\begin{array}{r}
47 \\
\text{(reversed)} \quad + 74 \\
\hline
\text{(total)} \quad 121
\end{array}
$$

If you don't get a palindrome the first time, repeat the process:

$$
\begin{array}{r}
19 \\
+ 91 \\
\hline
110 \\
+ 011 \\
\hline
121
\end{array}
$$

Try it with these numbers: 68, 69, 79.

You'll find that very few numbers require more than six steps to produce a palindrome, until you come to 89 or 98. You can try these numbers if you wish, but be warned: it takes twenty-four steps to reach the palindrome. Furthermore, I should stay away from the number 196 if I were you. It hasn't actually been proved yet that every single number treated in this way *will* eventually produce a palindrome. Computers have taken the number 196 through several thousand stages and still haven't come up with a palindrome, but that doesn't mean that they never will . . .

# What's the Point in a Million Points?

To end this chapter, here's a problem to make you think. Imagine a circle, inside which there are a million dots. If you joined every single dot to every other single dot by a straight line running right across the page, you'd have an enormous number of straight lines. The question is, would it be possible to draw a new straight line across the circle, without touching a single dot, dividing the million dots *exactly* in half with 500,000 on one side of the line and 500,000 on the other side?

Well, the answer is, in theory, yes you could. Here's the proof. The circle would be very full of lines, but as you got further from the centre of the circle, you would find a little space through which no line had passed. OK. Let's assume we have found a space. Make a dot

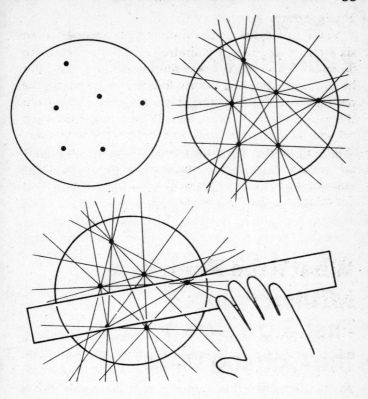

in this space. Now this new dot cannot be in line with any other two dots, otherwise there would be a line through it already. So, by laying a ruler through this dot, and sweeping the ruler slowly round and across the circle, it should be possible to sweep past the dots one at a time, until you have swept past 500,000. At that moment, if you drew a line along the ruler, it would divide the million dots exactly in half . . . Doing it is another problem.

# CHAPTER 4

# Plain Paper Planes

The idea of this chapter is to make plain paper planes, or, rather, paper planes from plain paper. But that doesn't mean that the plane designs will be plain – oh, no. If our paper planes were plain, you'd have every right to complain, but it will become plain, as each plane is explained, that the plane designs are anything *but* plain. It's the paper you use that should be plain. I hope that is quite plain.

## First, Slow Down the Coming Down

Air is a fluid just like water, and it flows and moves around in similar ways. In air, objects either sink (if they're heavier than air) or rise up (if they're lighter). I'm sure you have seen balloons filled with helium, which when released fly up into the air until they are so high you can hardly see them. Well, those balloons keep on rising until the density inside the balloon and the surrounding air are equal. You can prove this next time you get a helium balloon. First, take the balloon indoors – otherwise when you release it you'll need a helicopter to get it back. OK. Find some pieces of card and tie them to the string attached to the balloon, making sure the card is heavy enough to make the balloon sink to the floor. Next, get a pair of scissors and snip bits off it. Not off the balloon, silly . . . snip bits off the card. After some trial and error, you will be able to make the balloon's density (that's its weight, compared to its volume) exactly the same as the surrounding air, and the balloon will hang motionless, suspended in mid-air.

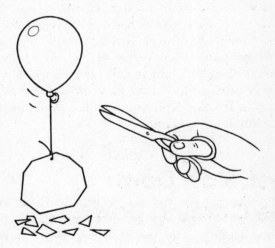

# Many Happy Returns

With all paper aircraft, the main problem is stopping the paper from sinking through the air too quickly. One way is to trap a cushion of air underneath the craft. This is how a frisbee flies. You can make an indoor frisbee from upside-down paper plates; stick a few together for the best results.

Launch your frisbee with a tennis back-hand movement, by giving your wrist a flick as you release the frisbee, causing it to spin. Thrown at an angle, the frisbee behaves as if it were on a slippery slope, and slides down a cushion of air as it loses speed. You will find that by altering the angle of launch, you can control whether the frisbee flies straight or curves to the left or right.

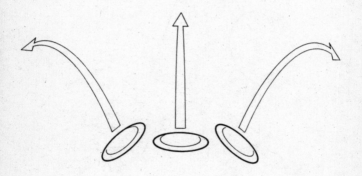

If you launch the frisbee away from you at an upward angle of about sixty degrees, it will eventually reach a stalling height and then slide through the air and return to you, arriving back at a point slightly lower than the one from which it was launched. Getting it to do this takes a bit of practice.

# Send Yourself a Card

The same principle can be used to perform a boomerang card trick. Hold a pack of cards in your left hand and push the top card sideways so that it overhangs the pack. Hold it in position very lightly with the left thumb, and then flick the bottom right-hand corner with your right index finger. If you hold the pack so that the card takes off at an upward angle of about forty-five degrees, it will spin away and then loop round and fly back. With practice, you will be able to catch it every time.

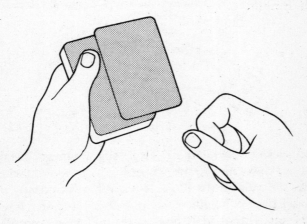

As well as boomerang card tricks, boomerang hat tricks can be performed with Mexican or Chinese straw hats. Thrown at the correct angle, they will fly back and land on your head.

# Downward Spirals

Just as spin helps frisbees and boomerangs to fly, so spin is used by Mother Nature herself to slow down the downward speed of her ingenious 'one-wing flying machine' – the sycamore seed. It works rather like a boomerang or frisbee, in that it depends on its centre of gravity being in the right place – except that with the sycamore seed, the right place is up at one end instead of in the middle. Try making a paper sycamore seed, and you'll discover for yourself how it works. First, trace and cut out your sycamore wing shape. Then cut out two pieces of thin card the shape of the shaded area

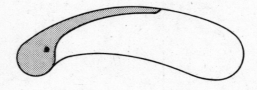

and stick one on each side of the wing. If you get it right, you will have moved the centre of gravity to somewhere near the 'dot' in the illustration. When you drop your model from a height, it should descend quite slowly, spinning round very fast with the wing spiralling through the air.

A simpler slow-descending, spinning craft can be made with any old piece of paper. Tear off a piece about three times as long as it is wide and you are ready to make a 'rotocopter'!

First, copy the dotted, dashed and solid lines – as in our diagram opposite – on to your piece of paper. Then cut or tear along the solid lines, fold forward along the dotted lines and backwards along the dashed line. Finally, fold the bottom end up in half. Now drop it from a height and watch it spin as it descends. If you've made it decently, it should be a very decent descent.

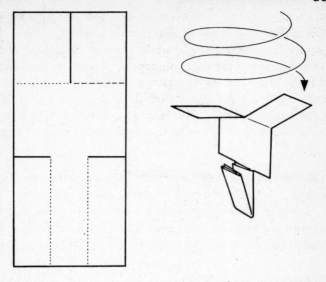

# Aerodynamics . . .
# a Blow-by-blow Account

Isaac Newton is said to have discovered gravity when he saw an apple fall to the ground. Here is an experiment with two apples which helps explain why aeroplanes don't do the same thing. Attach two apples to pieces of cotton and hang them side by side, about 5 cm apart. Now blow hard between the apples and watch what happens. You might expect the apples to be blown further apart, but, as soon as you blow, you see them swing in towards each other. Why?

Well, it's due to something called the Bernoulli effect, which states that moving air has less pressure than still

air, and that the faster air moves, the more the pressure drops . . . But how does that make an aeroplane fly?

Try this experiment. Take a strip of paper and stick it to your bottom lip. (You may have to hold the paper in place on your lip.) Now blow. What happens to the

paper strip? It rises up into a horizontal position. This is because the air you blow over it is moving quite fast and is therefore at very low pressure, while the air underneath the strip is at normal, and therefore higher, pressure. The greater pressure underneath pushes the paper upwards.

The heaviest aircraft ever weighed 379.9 tons at take-off. Now surely the difference in pressure above and below the wing can't be strong enough to keep all that weight up in the air . . . Well, with the assistance of the forward thrust of the engines, it is and it does. In fact, you yourself can use your breath to reduce pressure and cause solid metal to be sucked up into the air. Try this.

Crouch down so that your mouth is level with a table-top. Now take two coins: place one near the edge of the table and the other one just behind it. Hold the nearer coin in position with one finger from each hand, and blow hard over the top of the two coins. A strong blow will reduce the pressure above the coins, causing the further coin to lift. Immediately, high-pressure air will rush in underneath it and the coin will blow away quite sharply.

In this way variations in pressure can lift an aircraft into the sky and keep it there; and by using flaps on the rear edge of the wings, the pressures can be adjusted to control the aircraft in flight. Now that you understand this, you will be able to build 'control' into your plain paper planes.

# Darts the Way To Do It

The easiest plain paper plane you can make is a dart; I've found that the following design works flightfully well. Take a piece of A4 paper and fold it lengthways down the middle. Open it out again and fold two corners into the centre line. Then fold the two new edges into the centre line as well. Now turn the model over and fold the two sides the other way to the centre line. Fold the whole thing down the centre line again – and there is your dart! Snip off the pointed nose (it's safer that way) and you are ready for a test flight.

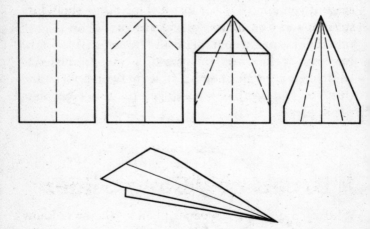

The dart is remarkably stable in flight because of the keel. If your dart tilts to one side as it flies, air escapes from under the upper wing, while air is caught under the lower wing. This causes a difference in pressure which pushes the lower wing up until both wings are

level and the pressure is equal again. So it usually flies quite straight. The distance it flies depends on weight distribution along its length. Attach a paper clip somewhere around the middle of the keel and fly the dart. Then move the clip backwards or forwards along the keel until you get the best results. When you launch the craft, if you don't force it forward too fast it should fly straight and true across the widest room.

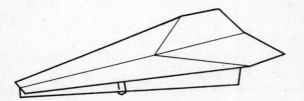

# A Brand-new Hang Glider

When you doodle with paper planes, you never know what you might discover. I've just found a way to make a pretty good hang glider model in just two minutes.

Take a piece of A4 paper and fold it down the middle lengthways, forming a keel. Secure the keel with a small paper clip at each end. Now fold two corners round to meet under the keel and fasten them together with

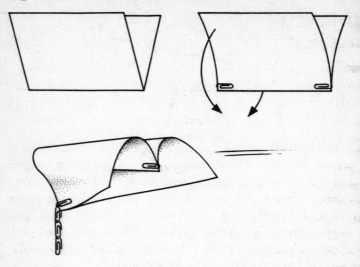

another paper clip. That's the model finished! Now all you have to do is to stabilize it by attaching about three more paper clips in a chain to dangle from the clip that holds the two corners. Hold it by the rear end of the keel, with the nose pointing slightly down, and push it forward gently to launch it. Watch it glide gracefully away, losing height quite slowly as it goes. I hope you like it as much as I did when I invented it.

# The Barnstorming Barnaby

Now I'm going to show you how to make a truly controllable aerobatic model. The design is based on a model called the Barnaby, after the American paper plane wizard who designed it while he was a teenager, some seventy years ago. All you need is a plain piece of

A4 paper. We need to build control into our model every step of the way – so here goes.

## Test Flight 1

Hold the paper by the long edge and drop it, watching what happens. The paper drops quickly, looping as it goes, completely out of control. O K?

First we need to give our model a leading edge. Whenever you are making a model that you want to control, you must remember to be very neat and accurate every step of the way. Fold one long edge of the paper over very carefully, making the fold 1 cm deep.

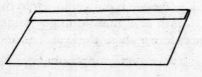

Now fold the fold over again. Continue folding the long edge over and flattening each fold out. Each time, flatten from the middle and then press evenly to each side. Stop when you have folded to about the middle of the paper. Your folds should still be square and you may need to make several attempts before you get a neat finish. Now turn the model over and, with one hand holding it flat, pull it over the square edge of a table-top, giving the unfolded part a slight upward curve. Then you are ready for . . .

# Test Flight 2

Hold the model by the middle of its rear unfolded edge and let it fall. This time, it should start to drop and then level out and fly quite a way. It will almost certainly veer off to one side, but this second flight is already quite smooth.

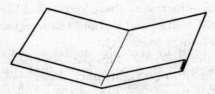

To stop it veering off, we need a keel (remember the dart and the hang glider). Very carefully, fold the model in half and open it out again. Hold the rear edge with your thumb and middle finger under the craft and your index finger above the keel. You are now ready for . . .

# Test Flight 3

Launch the model by pushing it gently away from you.
It will now fly a gentle switchback course, veering to
one side then the other.

Now we need a little more directional control, so
carefully fold the model in half and fold each wing tip
inwards by about 1½ cm.

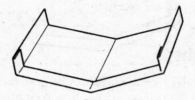

# Test Flight 4

With careful adjustment, these folds should keep it on a
dead straight course and it should descend with fewer
switchback bumps in its flight.

Now for the tricky bit. This part isn't difficult to do,
but it is difficult to get right, since a lot depends on the
weight of the paper you use and the weight of your
leading edge. Mark out a line, as shown in the diagram,

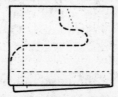

and then carefully cut along the line, once more making sure both sides of your craft are exactly the same. Then fold the tips of the tailplane out and down, but only a little. Make sure that the line of the fold points slightly towards the nose of the model. If you have done all this carefully, you are ready for . . .

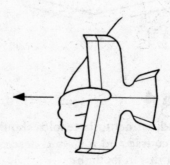

# Final Test Flight

First launch the model from the rear and try to get a straight, even flight. Never over-adjust between flights. The slightest change in a fold can produce quite a drastic change in performance. Once you have a straight, even flight, you are ready to build in aerobatic capabilities.

Hold the model by the nose and pull the tailplane through your finger and thumb, giving it a very slight upward curve. The curve must be the same on both sides. This should be enough to get your model to loop the loop. To launch it, this time hold it by the nose with the keel towards you, and pull it straight up in front of you sharply. It should loop up and over, returning to your hand.

After the up-and-over loop, you can try horizontal loops. With the same hold, draw the model sharply across your body and release it. With a bit of practice and slight adjustment to the wing tips, the craft should fly round in a circle and return to you. Do not over-adjust a model that flies well. It would be better to make copies of the design and keep a good flier to one side for future reference.

And finally . . . try the ultimate loop. Holding the craft by the nose, bring it sharply down in front of your body and release it. At incredible speed, it should dive, straighten, rise and complete a perfect loop. It might even go on to complete a second loop. When it does, you'll agree that it was well worth the effort.

# CHAPTER 5

# What Knots are not Knots?

If people who knit are called knitters and people who tie knots are called knotters, what do you call people who tie knots that are not knots? They are neither knitters nor knotters as they don't knot nothing (notting?). You could call them nits who do not knot knots, or even nutty not-knotters, but, whatever you call them, all knitters and knotters and even not-knot knotters are in fact *topologists*, as the science of knitting and knotting is all part of the branch of mathematics known as *topology*. How do you become a topologist? You could start as a bottomologist and work your way up, or you could

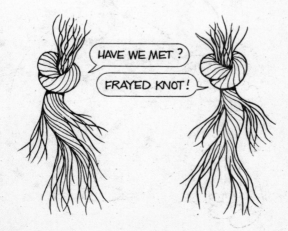

start by reading this chapter of topological twists and turns and knots and not-knots, if you've 'notting' better to do. Let's start by getting unknotted.

# Inside – Outside . . . Outside – Inside

For this trick, you need someone dressed in a 'body-warmer' or cycling safety jacket, or a sleeveless sweater or cardigan. Some of these garments are reversible, with one design on one side and a different design on the other. The question is, is it possible to turn the garment inside out without taking it off? Well, of course it is. First, tell your helper to clasp his hands in front of him. Then quickly draw the garment up over his head and down his arms so that it is over his hands. Then pull it

inside out through the arm-holes and slide it back up the arms and over his head – all in less than ten seconds. It's as easy as that. In fact, with three or four jackets you have the makings of a great party game. Pair your guests off, and give each pair one jacket. One person does the wearing and the other does the unravelling. Ready, steady, go!

# Unlooping the Loop

Find a sleeveless jacket with a pocket in it. Then find about one metre of rope or string, and make this into a long loop by tying the ends together. Ask your victim to put on the jacket and put one hand through the loop of string, then place his hand firmly in one of the jacket pockets. The problem is to remove the loop without untying the ends or the victim taking his hand from his pocket. On the face of it, it would seem to be impossible, but don't you believe it. Here's how you do it.

The loop of rope is pushed through the arm-hole of the jacket and over the victim's head. Then it is pushed through the other arm-hole and down over that arm. The loop can now be pulled back so that it circles the chest under the jacket, and it can easily be slid down the body and trousers to the floor. If the victim then refuses to step out of it, the whole loop can be lifted up over his body. 'S easy!

# Casting a Clout — Wrong Way About

There's an old English proverb that goes 'Ne'er cast a clout, till May be out', meaning don't take off your layers of winter clothing until summer has really arrived. These days we adjust for changes in temperature by wearing sweaters of different thicknesses, and it's difficult to imagine that sweaters were only introduced about fifty years ago. Until then, most men wore the same three-piece suit all the year round, with a button-up waistcoat under their jackets (the sort that snooker players still wear).

For a really terrific – but very old – party trick, you need to wear a waistcoat or a sleeveless sweater and, on top of that, a large man's jacket. The trick is to remove the waistcoat without taking off the jacket, and here's how to do it.

First, pull the jacket up from behind and over your head on to your arms. Then work the waistcoat up and over your head in the same way, and then pop the jacket back over your head into place again. The waistcoat will now be across your chest. You then work the arm-hole down the inside of the jacket sleeve and pass it over the arm and hand. Then pull the waistcoat back up that sleeve and push it down the other jacket sleeve, until you can pull it out of that sleeve from the bottom.

Remember this trick for when you are on holiday. If there's nowhere to change on the beach, it must be possible to swap your underpants for your swimming-trunks without taking your trousers off. Let me know how you get on!

# Hanky Panky

In the days before paper tissues arrived, everyone always carried a handkerchief and it always came in handy. For instance, if there was something you needed to remember, you could tie a knot in your handkerchief.

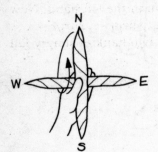
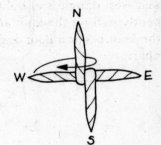

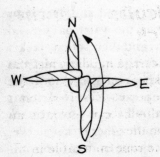

Well, here's a knot for anyone with two handkerchiefs, but nothing to remember.

Take one handkerchief by two diametrically opposite corners and twirl it round until it forms a rope-like shape. Do the same with the other handkerchief. Then lay one across your left hand (palm up) in an east–west direction and place the other across it in a north–south direction. Now take the north end and pass it down behind the west arm, and then bring it up in front pointing north again, and hold it with the left thumb. Next, take the west end and pass it up behind the north arm and back across the front to the west again. Hold that with the left thumb too. Now bring south up to north and hold them both in the right hand. Let east and west dangle and hold them in the left hand. Now gently pull on the knot and . . . surprise, surprise . . . the knot is not a knot and the two hankies simply fall apart.

## Handkerchief Handcuffs . . . or the Handkerchuffed Trick

Why does a policeman always carry a handkerchief? So that, if his whistle doesn't work, he can always blow his nose . . . if he has a piece of rope as well – How long? Oh, about one Scotland Yard – he can use it as an arresting method for making handcuffs.

To do this trick, first lay the rope on a table in 'Z'

formation. Then ask two young helpers to lift the ends of the rope off the table. (This makes them young off-enders, so keep your eye on them.) Ask them to place a finger in each angle of the 'Z' and pull the rope taut with their free hand.

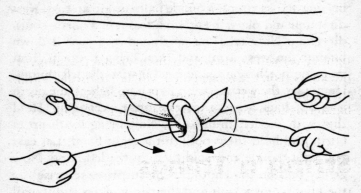

You then pass a rolled hanky under the three strands of rope. You bring the nearer end up, over the strands of rope, and to the left. Then the further end is lifted up, forward, over the other end, then under it and to the right, forming a knot. (N.B. There are two ways of tying a simple knot, one a mirror-image of the other. This trick will work only if the knot is tied in the correct way.)

Now push the two ends of the handkerchief down through the loops formed in the rope and tie the ends underneath in a double knot. You now have a pair of handcuffs, and if you place your hands through the loops and your helpers pull the rope ends, your hands will be handcuffed together. But here is the amazing bit: let your helpers loosen the loops so that you can get your hands out, then ask them to just pull the rope ends

tight. They will be amazed to discover that the hanky is
not knotted on the rope at all: it will fall to the floor and
they'll be left holding the rope! They'll probably have a
hankering to know how it's done. Don't tell them.

# String 'n' Things

Why do people like the mint with the hole? Once you've
eaten the mint, you never taste the hole. It must be the
sweet with the less fattening centre. In any case, here is
a wholesome trick you can perform with some holey
sweets and a stringy piece of string.

First, thread a sweet on to one end of the string. Then
hold the two ends together so that the sweet dangles
downwards. Now thread both ends through six or seven

sweets with holes in, so that they dangle on the string, held in place by the bottom sweet.

Next hang a hanky over the string and the sweets. Put your free hand beneath the hanky and, almost immediately, the threaded sweets are unthreaded and cascade to the floor. When you remove the handkerchief, everyone will see that you are still holding both ends of the string and one sweet is still dangling at the bottom. How did the other sweets come off it? Is it magic? Come off it. It's a trick, and here's how it's done.

When threading the seven sweets on to the pair of strings, you secretly make sure that the very last sweet is threaded on to only *one* string. Then, as soon as you cover the sweets with the hanky, you reach underneath and break the bottom sweet between your fingers. The threaded sweets then drop off, and you hide the broken sweet in your hand or pop it in your pocket. When the spectators see the single dangling sweet, they won't realize it's not the same sweet as the one you started with. Aaaah. Why don't you give the poor suckers a sweet each?

# The String and Ring Thing

To perform this thing, you need a loop of string and a ring, old thing. O K?

First, thread the loop of string through the ring and then pass the ends of the loop of string over your helper's thumbs. Now hook your left index finger round both strands of the loop at point 'X'. Then with your right hand, take the nearer string at point 'Y' and pull it forward and up, and over your helper's right thumb

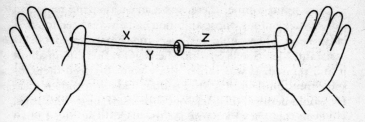

(that's the one to *your* left). Next, draw the ring to your left and then take the further string at point 'Z' and raise it up back, and to the left, and drop it over the same thumb from back to front.

Now ask your helper to bring her index fingers to her thumbs so that the string cannot escape her thumbs. Then take away your left hand and at the same time move the ring to the right with your right hand. To everyone's surprise, the ring is suddenly completely free of the string. Now, there's a thing!

# Sawing a Lady in Half

This is a clever method of sawing a lady in half, without making the lady sore by actually sawing her with a saw. To perform the trick, you need a drinking straw (to act as the lady) and a piece of string (to act as the saw). You also need a pencil and an elastic band or piece of sticky tape. Before you start, tie a small knot in one end of the string so you know which end is which, and fasten the pencil and the drinking straw together at one end with sticky tape or a rubber band. Like all performed tricks, this one is more entertaining if it is accompanied by a story . . . so here goes.

Once upon a time, there was a most amazing magician called Stu Pendous whose ambition had always been to saw a lady in half. The trouble was, every time he suggested it to his assistant, Miss Sheila Systim, Sheila got rather cut up about it and refused. It was rather a saw point between them for some time, until one day Stu Pendous had a stupendous idea. He would perform the trick, not with a saw, but with a rope. He even thought of a name for the trick: 'The Red Indian Rope Trick'.

At this point, you ask someone to hold the pencil and straw upright on the table and bend the straw forward out of the way.

That night, Stu went through his act until it was time for his big finish, and then he announced 'The Red Indian Rope Trick'. Stu walked to his totem pole and placed a rope across the front of it. The ends of the rope were passed round and crossed behind the totem pole, and crossed again in front of it.

Note: in doing this trick, always make sure that the same end – the knotted end if you like – crosses higher up the pencil than the other end.

Next, Stu asked his assistant, Sheila Systim, to stand in front of the pole and, quite unsuspecting, she did so.

Here the person holding the straw allows it to stand by the pencil again.

Then Stu crossed the two ends of the rope across the front of Sheila, passed them round the back of the totem pole, and then crossed them again in front of her once more.

Then, as the drum-roll began, two strong men from the audience began to pull on the ends of the rope. There was a loud gasp from the audience as the rope passed right through both the totem pole and the lovely Sheila.

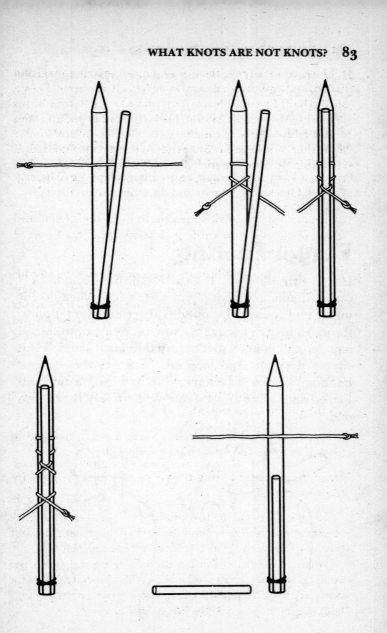

Here you pull on the string ends and the string pulls free, *but the straw is cut in half*.

Amazingly, the totem pole was completely unharmed, but what about Sheila? Well, she went all to pieces and immediately broke up her partnership with Stu. However, there is a happy ending, for Sheila is still in show business to this day. Last I heard, she was in pantomime, playing two halves of a cow. One half in Bognor and the other half in Aberdeen.

# Finger Fooling

Here's a simple trick. Take an elastic band and hook it round the index finger of your left hand. Then take it under and round your middle finger and loop it on to the index finger once again. Now ask someone to choose a finger and hold on to it to trap the elastic band. Then simply drop the end loop off the finger they are *not* holding. They will be amazed to find the elastic band looped on the free finger – completely free of the chosen one!

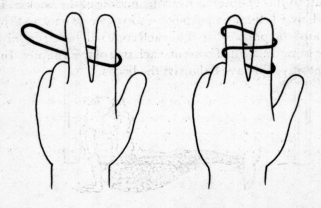

# CHAPTER 6

# In the Balance

Are you a scaley person? I don't mean, do you look like a haddock and breathe through your cheeks. By 'scaley', I mean are you one of those people who was born between 24 September and 22 October? If you are, because you were, then you are a scaley person because you were born under the sign of Libra and your zodiac symbol is a pair of scales.

Now, why should a pair of scales be used as a symbol for Libra? Well, it's because Libra begins on 24 September which is the autumn equinox, one of only two days in the year, half-way between mid-summer and mid-winter, when the length of the day and the night are equal and therefore balanced. In fact, I've plaiced this chapter as near the middle of the book as I cod, and I did it on porpoise – sorry, we're back to fish again – on purpose, so that each copy will have roughly the same amount of book on each side of this chapter. In that way, I'll have balanced the books.

# What is the Centre of Gravity?

It's the letter 'v', isn't it? What a 'v' old and 'v' awful joke, but gravity – and the centre of it – is very important when it comes to balance.

As proof of that, here's a way of finding the centre of gravity of any flat piece of card. First, find a piece of card and cut it into an irregular shape. In our TV programme, we used a map of Great Britain. We stuck the map on some cardboard and then cut it out. Then we stuck a nail into the map at a point very near to John o'Groats and hung the map from it – you could try the

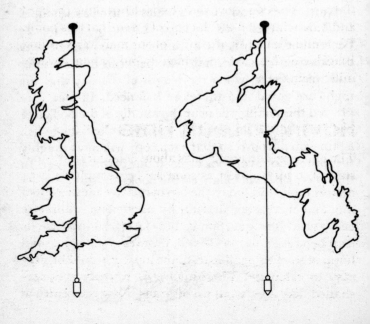

same thing. Also from the nail, we hung a plumb-line; that's a thread with a weight on the end – any weight will do to make a plumb-line, you could even use a plum (no you couldn't, it's too squashy). The weight will make the thread hang straight down, pointing 'plumb' to the centre of the Earth. Next we took a pencil and carefully traced a line, marking where the thread lay across the map. Then we took the map down and rehung it from another point on or near its edge. We chose a spot close to Land's End in Cornwall. When we let the plumb-line hang down across the map once more, the thread passed over our pencil line, and this time we marked the place where the second line crossed the first line. If all this is done carefully, the point where the two lines cross should mark the centre of gravity of the card. You can prove that this is so by taking the card and balancing it on the flat end of a pencil at this point. We found the centre of gravity of our map to be around Blackburn, Lancashire, which is only about twenty miles from the sea.

# Having a Lean Time

The Leaning Tower of Pisa is about 800 years old and it started to lean almost as soon as it was built. It is 54 metres high, and today the top of it is five metres out of line and increasing its lean by about one millimetre every year. The question is, how far can it increase its lean before it falls over? Well, if it were made of a solid lump of something, like iron, the answer would be very easy to calculate. The building is roughly cylinder-shaped, like a very tall tin of beans. Now the centre of

gravity of a full tin of beans is exactly half-way up and in the very centre of the tin. Try leaning a full unopened tin over, to see how far it will lean before it falls. The tin should lean over until just one point on the top rim of the tin is directly over the diagonally opposite point in the bottom — the point that is resting on the table. In this position, the centre of gravity is between the two points and also directly over the point touching the table, and the tin is more or less balanced — the slightest increase in lean and the tin will topple over.

Now the Tower of Pisa isn't a solid lump, it's a building made of stone blocks, so it can't lean over as far as a solid cylinder. In fact, the building is getting very close to the critical stage now. Soon the stress of leaning over will cause the individual stone blocks to be torn apart and the overhanging side will collapse . . . but when? Well, dozens of experts keep a constant watch on the tower and they will most certainly take action before a real possibility of collapse occurs . . . Ah, never mind.

Why don't you build a tower and see how far you can get it to lean without falling over? What you need are some dominoes or wooden bricks. Try to stack them into a leaning pile, so that no part of the very top piece is directly over any part of the bottom piece. It's more difficult than you think. In fact, with a pile leaning over 'evenly' it's impossible. The way to do it is to lay down

the first domino or brick, and then lay the second piece overlapping the first piece very slightly. Then lay the third piece overlapping a little more. The next piece can overlap a little more still, and so on, up the pile. At first, you will find you need about ten pieces to get the top piece overhanging the bottom piece completely, but with practice you may find that you are able to do it with only six pieces.

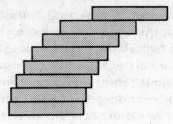

Is it possible to do it with five pieces? I don't know . . . but I do know that you can do the trick with five playing cards, by placing the bottom card edge to edge with a table and overlapping the other cards a bit more each time. Try it. You should be able to get the fifth card completely overhanging the table without it falling to the ground. It's easier with playing cards as they are lighter and, if they are perfectly flat, air pressure helps to hold them together.

# Corks 'n' Forks

What is a funambulist? Why, this chap is, of course. To make him, all you need is a cork, two forks and a dead matchstick. Carefully bore two holes into the small end of the cork, push half the matchstick into each, and

there are his two legs. The forks are then carefully stuck into the sides of the cork to form dangling arms. Draw his face with a felt-tip pen, and your funambulist is ready to funambulate. Tie a piece of cotton to a door-knob and, holding it taut, stand your little man on the thread by one leg and, sure enough, he'll balance. You can rock the thread gently from side to side or even slope it so that he slides backwards and forwards, but the little chap will stay balanced just like a real funam-bulist, which means tightrope walker. Bet you knew that, but do you know why he balances? It's because, due to the weight of the forks, his centre of gravity lies some way below the thread. To fall off, he would have to rock so far to the side that his centre of gravity would rise above the height of the thread.

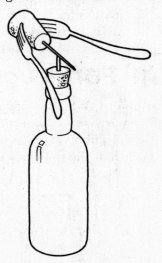

Now take his legs off and replace them with one long cocktail stick or even a pencil, and you will be able to find out exactly where his centre of gravity is. You need a bottle with a cork in it, and you must carefully bore a hole in this cork and stick a dead matchstick into the cork. With a little trial and error, your model will balance horizontally on the matchstick, and the centre of gravity of your funambulist is either at the point of balance or directly below that point.

# Platter Clatter

For this next trick you will need a metal or plastic plate, four corks (or four blobs of plasticine will do), a bottle with a cork and a matchstick stuck in it, and four forks. Carefully stick a fork in each cork and rest them on the edge of the plate so that all four forks have the same

angle of dangle. Then, feeling with your fingers, find the point of balance under the plate and balance the whole lot on top of the match on top of the bottle. Now, by blowing gently, you can get the plate and forks and corks to revolve round and round and round until . . . Crash! I *did* say use a tin or plastic plate, didn't I? Thank goodness for that.

# In Two Words – Im Possible

The great Hollywood film producer Sam Goldwyn is supposed to have said, when asked his opinion about something, 'In two words – im possible!' but, whether it's one word or two, these next three tricks really do seem im, poss and ible. What do you think?

First you need a rigid wooden ruler, a hammer and a loop of string. You'll find you can assemble them and get them to hang from the edge of a table in this 'impossible' way.

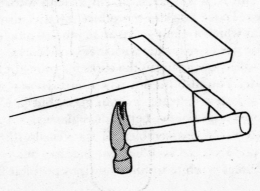

Next, ask if you can borrow some utensils from the kitchen, but remember, no sharp knives. I managed this 'in cred ible' trick using a bottle and a tin plate and two ladles with a hook on the end of their handles. It's amazing just what you can get to balance, if you try.

Thirdly, here is a very delicate balancing trick. It was a popular after-dinner trick in the olden days when table knives were made of silver with very heavy handles. Today you can reproduce the trick using two spatulas which are not sharp at all, and so much safer. You also need two bottles with sharpened corks . . . you might ask someone to cut the corks for you to be on the safe side. You also need a paper cup. In our picture we've shown a delicate cocktail glass, but you'll find that paper cups bounce better than glasses.

When you have assembled all the utensils, the whole contraption should look like our picture, but you will find it takes a while to find the right position for the

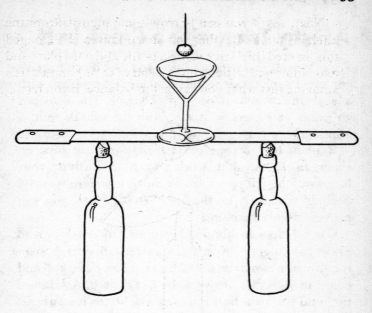

bottles and spatulas before you can get them to balance.
You may have to weight the handle end of the spatulas
with plasticine and adjust the amount of water in the
cup, but when it all balances, you are ready for the next
stage. (Slightly overlapping the spatulas also helps.)

Find a piece of thread and a small, but heavy, weight
(a blob of plasticine would do nicely). Now you will
find that if you dangle the plasticine in the water, it
increases the weight at the centre of the device and the
cup starts to go downwards. Quickly pull the plasticine
out again, and the cup will rise. With practice, you can
dip the plasticine in and out and the cup will bounce up
and down, up and down, until eventually . . . splash! I
told you to use a paper cup.

# A Fishy Trick with a Catch in It

For this trick, you need a fishing-rod, but if you haven't got any fishing tackle, you can tackle this problem with a bit of thread and a paper clip for a hook. You also need 30 mints or sweets with a hole in the middle, and a blindfold.

Explain to everyone present that you are such an expert fisherman that, when you catch a fish on your line, you can tell exactly how much it weighs, just by 'feeling' the strain on the line. What's more, you will prove it. How? Like this!

Get a helper to blindfold you and then ask him to draw his finger through the sweets, dividing them roughly into two halves. Ask him to choose one half and count the number of sweets he has chosen. Ask him if the total is a two-digit number, like 16 for instance. If the answer is 'yes', ask him to add the two digits together and take that number away from his pile. Now ask him to split the sweets he has left into two groups and to hook one group on to your paper clip hook. Concentrate very hard, 'feeling' the weight of the hooked sweets on the end of your 'line'. As a matter of interest, ask him how many sweets he has left in his group. When he tells you, you then announce how many sweets you think are on your hook. Remove your blindfold and, sure enough, you were right! Your helper will be standing there gaping like an incredulous codfish! But how did you do it? Simple.

With 30 sweets to start with, dividing them roughly in half will almost certainly produce two piles with between 10 and 19 in each pile. In fact, if the chosen pile doesn't have between 10 and 19 sweets in it, the trick won't work. Let's assume the chosen pile has 14 sweets in it. Ask your helper to add the digits and take that number away:

$$1 + 4 = 5 \qquad 14 - 5 = 9$$

That sounds fair enough, but you will find that, for any number from 10 to 19, this process will always result in nine being left. Once your helper has hooked some sweets on your line, you ask how many he has got left. Let's assume he says, 'Six.' All you need to do now is take that number away from nine, and then you know that there are exactly THREE sweets on your hook. When you announce the answer, you will have dumbfounded everyone, hook, line and sinker.

# Wacky Gravity Races

I remember once at school, our classroom idiot was disqualified from the egg and spoon race. The teacher had caught him sticking the spoon to his hand. Not eggzactly a clever thing to do. But anyway, for those who like silly races, here is a new one to try . . . or at least to try to try.

For each person in the race, you need two large balloons, and you must push one balloon inside the other, with the neck hanging out – before they have been blown up, of course. Now pour some water into the inner balloon until it is about the size of two fists, and then knot the neck. Push the inner balloon right inside the outer balloon and then blow that one up as far as it will safely go, and tie a knot in the neck. (The balloon's neck, not your own.) When you have got one of these double balloons for everyone, you are ready for the race.

Line everyone up at the start. They must balance their balloon on the back of one hand and put the other hand behind their back. On the word 'Go', they have to race to the finish, without dropping their balloon.

I call this the Wacky Gravity Race, as the racers will find it just about impossible to balance the balloons. You see, the centre of gravity is situated somewhere around the middle of the heavier water-filled balloon; however, because it rolls about so much inside the larger balloon, the centre of gravity is constantly moving, making it impossible to keep it balanced.

Once the race has been abandoned, you can try standing in a circle and throwing one of the double balloons across the circle from person to person. Every-one has three lives, after which they drop out. You'll find it very difficult to catch because the balloon flies through the air in such a lollopy way! Try it and see.

# CHAPTER 7

# Patience is a ...
# (I'll tell you later)

The other day, I woke up with a sick eye, so I thought I would have to go to see a sick-eye-atrist, but instead I went along to see my doctor (I realized I'd have to see him with the other eye until the sick one got better). While I was waiting for the doctor to see me (*his* eyes were perfectly O K), I noticed how long doctors keep people waiting in their waiting-rooms, but with everyone else I waited patiently and realized why patients are called patients.

Now if I had taken a pack of cards with me that day, while waiting patiently with the other patients I could have kept my patience by patiently playing 'Patience' – and if you can find a pack of cards, so can you.

In the past, parents have often frowned upon games of Patience as great time-wasters, but these days most people agree that games involving mental agility are very good for you. There are many different games of Patience, each requiring a different level of mental agility as well as varying degrees of skill and luck, so I'd better describe a few quickly, before you get tired of waiting and lose *your* patience.

# Idiot's Delight

In every Patience game, the position in which the cards are laid out is called the 'tableau'. In 'Idiot's Delight' the tableau is a simple row of four spaces.

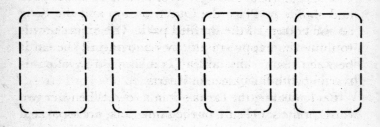

The object of the game is to discard or chuck out all the cards except the four Aces. Begin by dealing four cards in a row to form the tableau. If two or more cards are of the same suit, discard the lower ones (remember: Ace is high). Next, deal four more cards on to the cards (or the spaces) in the tableau, and once again discard the lower cards where cards of the same suit occur. If you are left with spaces in the tableau, you can move any top card into a space, and this should help you to discard more cards. Then deal four more cards and continue. Each round should end with just one card from each suit on top of the four piles, and after thirteen rounds, with luck, you should be left with just the four Aces. It's a very simple game and tends to come out more often than most games of Patience, which is why it's called Idiot's Delight. A little skill is involved in judging which top cards to move into spaces when they occur.

# Distant Hearts

This true love story concerns the desperate plight of two lovers and their fight to remove and overcome the vast obstacles between them so that they may at last find each other . . . Will they? It's all down to luck, innit?

Take the King and Queen of Hearts from the pack and shuffle it. Place the Queen on top and the King on the bottom of the shuffled pack. The object now is to unite the happy couple, by removing all the cards between them. The tableau is a simple row of cards starting with the Queen of Hearts.

Begin dealing the cards out in a row. Whenever two cards of the same suit, or the same rank, are separated by one or two cards, these intervening cards are removed and the row is closed up to the left. Each time you close up the row, check to see if there are any other cards that can now be discarded. If you are very very lucky, you will manage to discard fifty of the cards and the King and Queen of Hearts will at last be together, side by side, for the perfect happy ending. Ahhhhh.

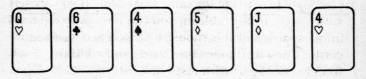

Here the two cards (Five of Diamonds and Jack of Diamonds) between the Fours go out. Then when the Four of Hearts is moved up, the Six of Clubs and Four of Spades go out.

# Accordion

This is probably the best of the single-row tableau games, but it's also the hardest to complete. Deal the cards in a single row from left to right. Whenever a card is the same rank or suit as the card immediately to its left or the card three places to its left, the right-hand card and all cards under it can be moved on to the other card. If the right-hand card matches *both* these cards, you can choose which of the two moves to make. After each move you must watch out, because new possible moves may have been opened up. As the game progresses, the line gets longer and shorter rather like an accordion, but the game is only complete if all the cards end up in one pile on top of the original first card. Sometimes this game is called 'Idle Year', because it hardly ever comes out.

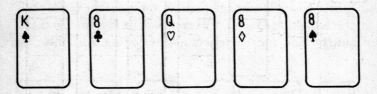

Here the Eight of Spades can go on the Eight of Clubs, then both can go on the King of Spades. But a better move is: Eight of Spades on Eight of Diamonds. Then both can go on the King of Spades. Then the Eight of Clubs moves on to the Eight of Spades.

To make it easier, after the first complete deal, you can gather the cards in the following way. Pick up the left-hand pile and, holding it face up, place the pile to its right on top of it. Continue in this way until the whole

pack is gathered up, then turn it over and try again.
Even this way, it's still very difficult – but that's half the
fun.

# Old Style ... New Style

The most widely known game of Patience is usually
called Klondike and it is laid out like this.

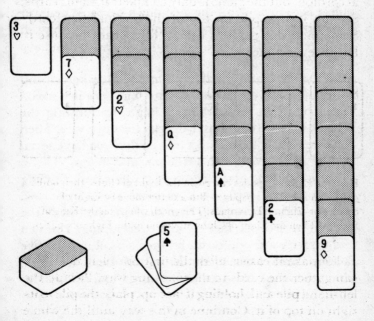

The seven face-up cards are 'in play' or 'available'. Available Aces are removed and set aside to form 'foundations'. Once an Ace has been set aside, the Two of the same suit can also be set aside and placed on top of the Ace, then the Three and so on. Other 'available' cards can be built on to, using a card the next rank down and of the opposite colour (so on top of a red Queen, you can place a black Jack and build down, red–black–red–black, etc.). Each time a face-down card is uncovered, it can be turned over and becomes 'available'. The rest of the cards form the 'stock', and these are dealt in threes on to a stock-pile. The top card of the stock-pile is also 'available' and can be moved on to the tableau or placed upon a foundation if it fits. The object is to turn up all the face-down cards. Whenever one of the seven columns becomes vacant, a King can be moved into the space, along with any cards that have been built on top of it.

As I said, this is probably the most widely known and commonly played Patience game, but here is a variation that I like much better. Begin by forming the tableau of seven columns in exactly the same way. Then close up each column into a pile, so that you have seven piles in a row, each with a face-up card on top.

Now leave the first face-up card alone and, starting on the second card, deal six more cards in a row, face-up and overlapping, then deal out the rest of the pack in rows of six, face-up and overlapping. You will end up with a single card and then six columns of five face-up cards. Once again the bottom cards are available, and available Aces are set aside to form foundations.

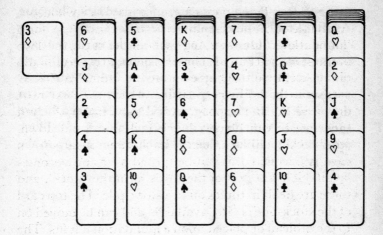

Other available cards can be built on, but only in this particular way: a card (say the Nine of Hearts) can only be built on with the next lower card of the same suit (that is, the Eight of Hearts), and only if that particular card can be seen in the tableau. When it is moved, all the cards overlapping it come with it, keeping their order.

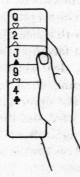

When face-down cards are uncovered, they become available too. When a column becomes vacant, a King can be moved into it, along with all the cards that are overlapping it. This system of moving groups of cards can lead to quite long columns, all of which must overlap so that all face-up cards can be seen. The skill in the game lies in checking several moves ahead before each move is made, because some moves will block other possible moves, due to key cards ending up in the same columns.

# Pyramid

Here is a Patience game that is great fun; it has a method of scoring, so you can play against yourself or another player. The tableau is a pyramid of twenty-eight cards laid out as in the diagram. During the game a card is available if it is not overlapped by any other card, so that at the beginning the seven cards in the bottom row are available. The rest of the cards are dealt one at a time on to a single waste-pile, the top card of which is also always available. The idea is to discard pairs of cards that add up to thirteen. Kings are discarded immediately they become available, counting as thirteen on their own. Queens count as twelve and can be discarded if paired with an Ace. Jacks must be paired with a Two, Tens with a Three, and so on. Once the waste-pile has been dealt out it can be turned over and redealt twice more.

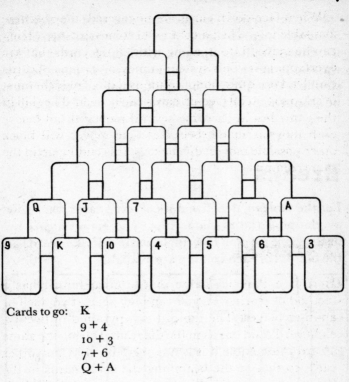

Cards to go:  K
9 + 4
10 + 3
7 + 6
Q + A

If the pyramid is removed completely on the first deal, score 50 points less the number of cards left in the waste-pile. If the pyramid is removed on the second deal, score 30 points less the remaining waste cards. Remove the pyramid on the third deal, and you score 20 points less the cards left in your hand. Failure to remove the pyramid after three deals counts as a minus score, scoring one point for each card in either the pyramid or the waste-pile.

Skill is required in choosing the best card when alternatives are available. A bad choice will often block the game. It also helps to remember the order of the waste-pile for the next deal, and this pile must not be shuffled. With practice and luck, you should on average be able to achieve a 'plus' score over a set of six games.

# Breaks

For the tableau, deal five rows of seven cards, each row overlapping the previous row. The game begins by dealing one card on to a single waste-pile. The cards at the bottom of each column are available.

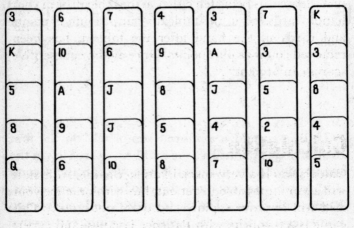

The idea is to clear away the tableau by building available cards on to the waste-pile. Building is done in sequence either up or down, but not circular (only a Two can be built on to an Ace and only a Queen on to a King). During each 'break', the sequence can be reversed as you require, so that in our example there are two ways of playing to the Nine: 10, J, Q, J, 10, or (better still) 8, 7, 6, 5, 4, 5, 4. After either of these 'breaks', the next card is dealt on to the waste-pile and play continues. Whenever a column becomes vacant, any available card can be moved into the space, allowing the card that was beneath it to become available. With clever play, long breaks can be built up.

It's quite surprising how often this game ends with just a few cards being left either in the tableau or in your hand. Cards left in the tableau count as minus points and cards in the hand after the tableau has been removed count as plus points. Once again, competitive scores can be kept.

# Calculation

Calculation is a very special Patience game. At first, it will seem impossible to get out, but with practice your skill will improve rapidly and quite noticeably. This game is a favourite with Patience fanatics, and expert players claim they can make it come out twice out of every three attempts.

The best way to explain the game is to start at the end. The game should end up with four piles of cards in

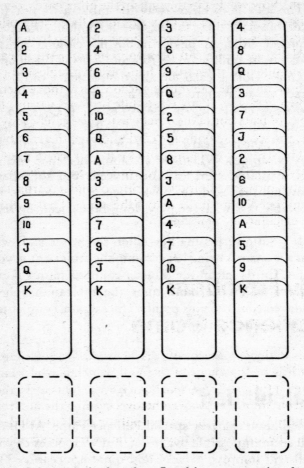

a special numerical order. In this game, suits don't count at all.

To start, you select any Ace, Two, Three and Four and place them in a row. These are your foundations, and you must try to build the rest of the cards on top of them. Now you begin turning up the other cards, one at a time, and placing them in *any* of the four waste-piles. These piles should be spread downwards so that all the cards in each pile can be seen. The top card in each waste-pile and the card in hand are available and can be built on to the foundations according to the sequence shown opposite. If any waste-pile becomes vacant, the top card from one of the other waste-piles can be moved into the space, making the card underneath available.

The secret of the game is to build four waste-piles so that the right cards become available when you want them, and they don't get trapped under cards that aren't needed until the end of the game. That's where the calculation comes in.

# My Favourite Patience Game

This Patience game hasn't, as far as I know, got a name, but it is my favourite of them all, which is why I have saved it till last. First, deal out a row of eight cards, then deal out another row of eight, overlapping the first row. Continue with further rows until the cards are all dealt out. The last row will have only four cards in it and you will end up with four columns of seven cards and four columns of six cards. The bottom card of each column is available. Aces, when available, are placed above the tableau to form foundation piles which are built up in suit order. Below the tableau are four temporary spaces for single cards only. Only one card is moved at a time.

Available cards can be moved on to the foundation piles if they will go, or on to another available card if it is the next highest card in the same suit (the Nine of Hearts, say, on to the Ten of Hearts) or into one of the four temporary spaces, where they remain available. If a column becomes empty, any available card can be moved into it. The fascination of this game is that every

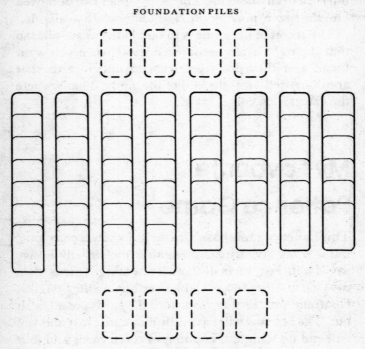

FOUNDATION PILES

TEMPORARY SPACES

card is on view from the start and, rather like a game of chess, it is possible to plan many moves ahead. In fact this is what you *must* do, as any careless move will cause the game to be lost. It's a good idea to use the temporary spaces to release the Aces early on, but as the game progresses you will often need to move cards in and out of the temporary spaces. If you are good at this game the chances of success seem to be about fifty-fifty; but to become good at it, you will need practice, dedication and a lot of patience.

# CHAPTER 8

# Illusionarioptics

If you've ever had an operation, you'll know that when it's healing up, it doesn't half tickle. In fact hairs down your neck or ants in your pants are nowhere near as ticklish as the tickle you get when your 'op' is healing up. Of course, if you've never had an operation, you can only try to imagine how fiendishly ticklish an after-operation tickle really is . . . go on . . . try it. Try to imagine that you have the most excruciating tickle and that you can't scratch it in case you damage your operation. Isn't it terrible – but don't worry, it's not real . . . what you have just had is only an Op Tickle Illusion – and that is what this chapter is all about.

# As Easy as Standing on Your Head

Illusionarioptics is all to do with seeing things that aren't really there, or seeing things happen that aren't really happening, and it's all about eye trickery. Eyes, you see, are very tricky things, because although we use them to see, we don't really see things as we think we see them, see? Here's a drawing of an Eye Ball . . . by J. Ball. You can see that rays of light from an object

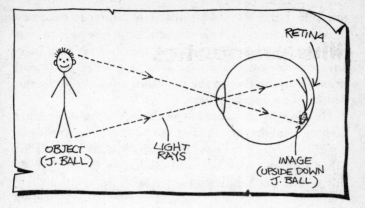

RETINA

OBJECT
(J. BALL)

LIGHT
RAYS

IMAGE
(UPSIDE DOWN
J. BALL)

pass through the front of the eyeball and land on sensors on the retina (so called because it's retina back of the eye). However, the rays of light entering the eyeball all cross over before hitting the retina, so that the eyeball actually sees things upside down. Our brain then has the job of flipping everything over so that we can see it the right way up. You don't believe me? Well, to prove it, here is a flipping image, or rather an image-flipping experiment. You need a pin and a piece of card with a

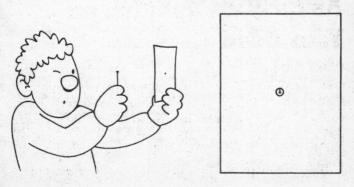

pin-hole in it. First hold the card up, about 10 cm away from your eye. Now hold the pin, head upwards, about half-way between the card and your eye. With a little adjustment you should be able to see the pin head 'framed' in the hole in the card but, amazingly, the pin head will be upside down.

Here's why it happens. Because the light rays are coming straight through a small pin-hole, they produce a right-way-up image on the retina but, as with all the other images, your brain immediately flips it upside down, and that's how you see it, see?

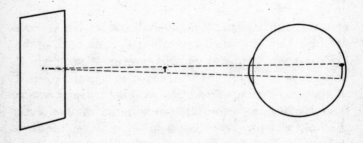

# Two Blind Spots

While on the subject of eyeballs, did you know that each of your eyes has a blind spot? Well, it has. You see, light information flashed on to the retina is picked up by nerves which carry messages to the brain. All these nerves are like so many very fine hairs, and they are gathered up in a bunch at the back of the eye, rather like a pigtail. At the point where they are gathered there is a small dimple on the surface of the retina and this point doesn't register any light at all.

To find this blind spot, close your left eye and gaze at

the dot on the left, below. By moving the book, or your head, first nearer and then further away, you will find a point where, while you are still gazing at the left dot, the right one disappears. Still looking at the left dot, try to find the right dot with your finger nail, and you'll find that that disappears as well.

Now try the whole experiment closing the right eye and gazing at the right dot. This time the left dot will disappear and you will have found both your blind spots.

● ●

# Eyes Right, Yous Left

Have you ever wondered why God gave us one mouth and one tongue and one belly-button, but two eyes? Perhaps he was worried that one wouldn't be able to see far enough? That can't be it, because even people who are short-sighted can see the sun with either eye, and that's 93,000,000 miles away. No, no. God gave us two eyes so that by using them together, we could see in three dimensions, and we do it pretty well. However, did you know that one eye always does more work than the other eye? Those who knew that, shout 'eye'. Those who didn't . . . eye will show u.

First of all, take two sheets of paper and make two paper tubes. Use the tubes like telescopes, one to each eye, and train them on two separate pages of a book or newspaper. You will find that you can get your brain to read the information seen by either eye, without closing the other one – which means that your eyes work independently and your brain selects the information from either eye, as it thinks fit.

OK, so which eye do you use most? Try this . . . Choose an object a little distance away – a door handle or a clock face – and play Cowboys and Indians. Make your hand into a gun with first and second fingers as the barrel . . . ready . . . set . . . DRAW – and shoot the distant object. Now keep your 'handgun' aimed at the object and close first one eye and then the other. You will find that in aiming your 'handgun' you actually sighted up with one eye only. Your brain immediately concentrated on the eye you use most. Which was it? Well, most people are right-eyed (eyed have thought you knew that) in about the same proportion as they are right-handed and right-footed.

Now here's a way to make a hole in your hand . . . not with a gun. Take one of your paper tubes and, using it as a telescope, try reading that book or newspaper

again, with one eye. Mask your other eye with the flat of your hand held next to the tube, some 15 cm away from your eye. With both eyes open you will find that you seem to be reading through a hole in your hand. It must be another optical illusion, as the hole in your hand didn't need an operation.

# Let's See What Isn't There

Take a look at this white square. It's lying on top of a black square and four black circular discs. Can you see it? You can? That's amazing, because it isn't there. All your eyes can see is some broken lines and four discs, each with a wedge missing; but because of the way they are arranged, your brain is making more of the picture and 'inventing' a white square to make the shapes make sense.

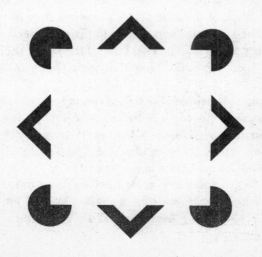

In fact, if you look at this next diagram, you will see a sort of white square with concave sides. Once again, the white shape isn't really there, but you can see it because of the shape of the four discs. This time they have been positioned a little further out and the wedge cut into them is narrower. The effect is still the same, though. It makes you see something that isn't there in the first place.

Using this principle of just giving a little information and making people's brains do the rest of the work, sign-writers could save a fortune in paint by drawing 'shadow letters'. For instance, can you make anything out of the lines at the top of page 121?

Although some are more obvious than others, they are all the letter 'E' written in shadow style. Think what 'THINK' would look like if we gave it the same treatment.

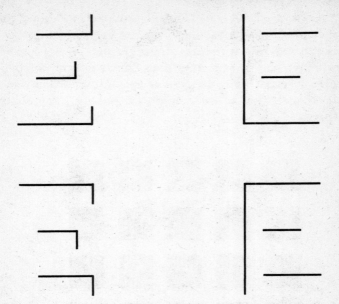

Once again, in each case, the brain is asked to fill in the missing information and it does so without any trouble whatsoever. In fact, sometimes the brain will add information when it is not needed at all.

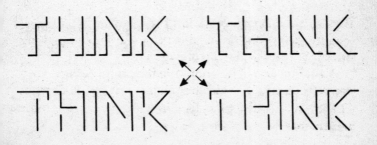

Look at this array of black squares for about 30 seconds. Lo and behold, there, at each junction between four black squares, a grey square will appear, whether you want it to or not. This is a sight for sore eyes, because your eyes create this mirage when they become tired or at least bored with looking at the same thing.

Eyes are stimulated by light. If they are confronted with black and white images, they tend to make more of the light and less of the dark areas. This explains why, of these two footballers, one appears thinner than the other. Which one? See for yourself and tell me . . . the white one seems larger and the black one smaller, because the brain tends to spread the white areas and reduce the black areas.

This effect is best illustrated by taking a long lingering look at this black cross. Notice what happens after staring at it for a while. The arms of the cross seem to shorten as though the flag had dents or kinks in its sides where the black areas were. Kinky, isn't it?

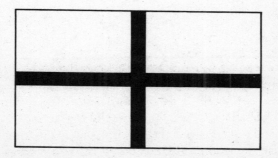

# Mind-bending Illusions

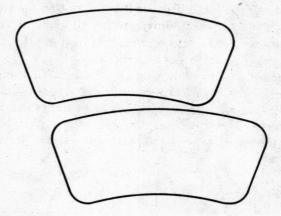

Of these two shapes, which one is the larger? Who said they are both the same? Bad luck. In truth, although the bottom one looks bigger, it is the top one that is slightly larger. If you don't believe me, get a ruler out and measure them. You are going to need a ruler anyway, but I have provided one for you in this next

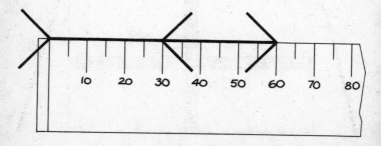

diagram. (Trouble is, rather like Richard III, it appears to be a bad ruler.) Here you see a line 6 cm long with other lines joining it at an angle. This is known as a 'distortion figure', because it has distorted the ruler so that the three centimetres on the left look longer than the three centimetres on the right. But are they? Why not get your own ruler and check?

While you're at it, you could check on these two rulers. Now with all rulers, centimetres are usually the same size, but, in this case, they don't seem to be. It's all because of the two lines that tend to converge. Now, is the top ruler bigger, or the bottom ruler smaller, or are

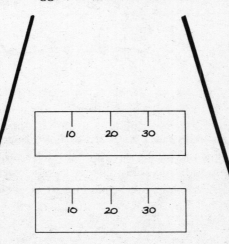

they both the same? It stretches the imagination, doesn't it?

Well, this next diagram is positively mind bending.

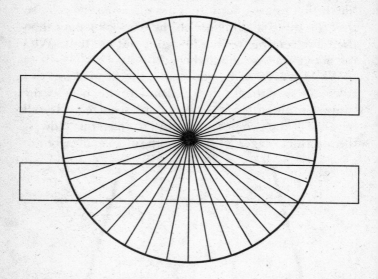

Once again, the ruler appears to have been altered. Rulers are straight, as a rule, but these two appear decidedly bent, and yet both are as straight as an arrow – which is more than can be said for these arrows . . .

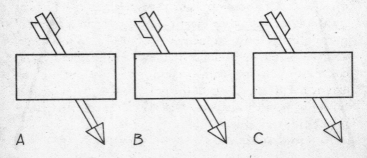

Which arrow follows the straight and narrow? Only one of them. When you have made your guess, hold the book up and look straight along the arrows to find the answer.

It's a funny thing about squares, but they all have square corners. In fact, if the corners of a square aren't square, neither is the square square, so what about these two squares?

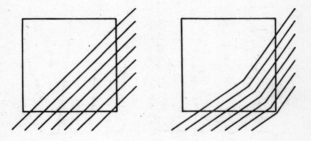

The left-hand square is definitely square, but the right-hand square doesn't seem square at the bottom right-hand corner.

You could make a distortion machine for yourselves and watch the distortion take place before your very eyes. You need some pins or tacks to form two lines at right angles and some elastic bands to form a series of parallel lines, as in our drawing. Then draw a square on a piece of paper and lay it under your elastic band contraption. Now, with a comb, you can pull on the elastic bands, bending all the parallel lines, and see just how the square distorts. Dist'ort to keep you out of mischief for a while.

And so should this:

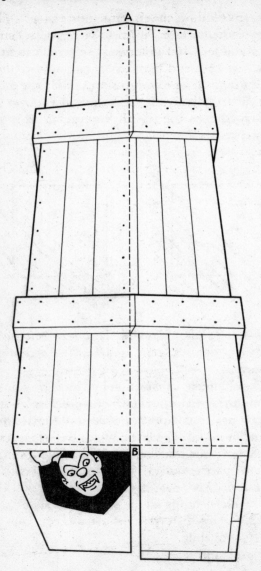

It's a friendishly clever three-dimensional illusion. Trace the diagram on to a piece of paper and cut it out carefully. Then fold it forward down the centre line A–B. Fold both end-flaps over, making sure the plain flap overlaps the one with the face. Hold the model by the small flaps between the finger and thumb of your left hand, and gaze at it with one eye until it appears to be a real three-dimensional box. Now by rubbing your left finger and thumb together, the box can be made to open slightly, revealing the dreaded Count Dracula. Don't worry, you can shut the box again before he has time to get out – fangfully!

# Moving Experiences

Did you hear about the lighthouse-keeper who ran up his spiral staircase so fast, he screwed himself into the ceiling? Spirals are funny things, and they are great for producing optical illusions that actually move. Take a strip of paper and wind it round a pencil in a spiral fashion and stick down the end.

Now when you roll the pencil along a flat surface, the spiral will appear to move along the pencil, with one end seeming to grow longer and the other end apparently growing shorter. You can get a similar 'mobile' effect if you draw a spiral on a round piece of paper and then cut along the spiral. You should end up

with a long snaky shape. Hang it on a pencil point and gently blow it, so that it revolves. You can also hang these snakes on threads near radiators and they will spin merrily all by themselves. But notice, as it spins, that the snake appears to be moving downwards.

Drawing spirals is quite easy and very satisfying. Try

drawing one and then placing it on a revolving record turntable, and you will experience another spiral illusion. Turntables always revolve clockwise, and if you have drawn your spiral clockwise, as it spins it will draw your eye inwards, looking as though it is all the time shrinking towards its centre. Draw your spiral anti-clockwise, and the spinning design will always appear to be growing outwards.

However, you don't need a record turntable to get this drawing to revolve. Just hold the book and move it

around in small circles as if you were spinning a ballbearing in a saucer. With practice you will be able to get the six dots spinning like ballbearings in a saucer. But what about the inner cogwheel? Quite amazingly that will start to spin in the opposite direction!

# CHAPTER 9

## HIDDEN SECRETS

This is a chapter on codes and ciphers, which is why it's called 'Hidden Secrets' and why 'secrets' is secreted (or hidden) behind 'hidden' in the title. Of course, we could have hidden the secret of the title more craftily or confusingly by printing it like this:

### S H E I C D R D E E T N S

Here, we have simply taken the letters from each word alternately, but even though the letters are still in their correct order, the result looks nothing like 'hidden secrets'. This just shows how easy it is to confuse people by jumbling up a few letters. Have a go at solving this similar little problem:

### N S U I M X L E B T E T R E S R S

Can you take six letters away and leave an English word you might associate with me? If you're stumped, turn to page 150 for the answer.

This messing about with letters and words in order to confuse or hide a meaning is called ciphering. There are many many ways of making a cipher, as you will 'cipher yourself' if you read on.

# Play on Words

Some people don't actually need to resort to ciphers to confuse other people; their hand-writing is so bad that no one can read it anyway! My own hand-writing is a bit like that. They say that the reason why many creative people write badly might just be that they subconsciously *want* to keep their writing secret.

You already know that Leonardo da Vinci wrote backwards (see Chapter 3), but perhaps you didn't know that both Samuel Pepys and Charles Dickens wrote using a simple form of shorthand, in which all unnecessary vowels (a, e, i, o and u) were missed out. Using this system, a typical sentence might look like this:

'Aftr fnshng my crspndnc, wlkd to dpndbl rstrnt nd dnd on rst bf flwd by an exclnt rbrb nd cstrd.'

There are many ways of playing around with letters to produce artistic effects. For instance, can you read this small word, which – amazingly – reads the same upside-down?

Some years ago, there was a racehorse called POTOOOOOOOO. If you don't get it, count the number of 'O's after 'POT', and you get POT-8-Os or POTATOES. Now you can try solving these, and perhaps even make up some of your own.

SUROROROROROR (one who lives to tell the tale)
TTTTFIED (usually a castle is this)
MENMENMENDOUS (a very large plant)
ISISISISISISISISISIS (service with a smile?)

Another good wheeze is to take words containing numbers and add one to each number, using the words to make up a story, something like this:

Once upon a time, there was an inn in Sevenoaks called The Five Foresters where the daily Mail Coach and four would stop while travellers ate a three-course meal for five and sixpence before going forward towards their destinations. Unfortunately, the atmosphere was forbidding and people attending thought nought of the place, until the benign tenant landlord hired a poet to cheer up the diners by relating a story as they ate. Before very long, the poet found himself at sixes and sevens, as his listeners tended to be the same ones every night. So, with great fortitude, he found a way of altering his single story by simply adding one to each number in the tale. Here is the tale he tentatively related:

Twice upon two times, there were two inns in Eightoaks called the Six Five-esters where the daily Mail Coach and five would stop while travellers nined a four-course meal five six and sevenpence, befive going fiveward threewards their destinations. Unfivetuninely, the atmosphere was five-bidding and people atelevending thought one of the place, until the beten elevenant landlord hired a poet to cheer up the diners by rel-nine-ing a story as they nined. Befive very long, the poet found himself at sevens and eights as his lis-eleveners elevended to be the same twos every night. So, with great fivetitude, he found a way of altering his double story by simply adding two three each number in the tale. Here is the tale he eleventatively rel-nined:

Four-fold upon four times, there were four inns in Tenoaks . . .

# Follow the Code

There are many ways of communicating with someone, other than writing or speaking to them. Symbols can be used to represent letters or words, and all systems using symbols come under the general heading of 'codes'.

A traffic policeman uses a simple system of hand-signals which can be immediately understood by anyone; and the deaf use a sign-language involving subtle hand-signals, though this is much more complex and users must spend some time studying and learning the code. On a racecourse, the tick-tack men keep one another informed of the changes in the betting, so that the odds against each horse can be adjusted to make sure the bookmakers have a slight advantage at all times.

A system similar to the tick-tack code was the use of flags. The Greeks used them; and up to a hundred years ago a flag code called semaphore was used for short-distance communications between ships or armies.

Semaphore can also be written, using the angular

A B C D E F G H I J K L M

N O P Q R S T U V W X Y Z

shapes to represent the letters. For numbers, a single 'J' is used, followed by the letters A to I for 1 to 9, and the letter K for 0. As an example, semaphore flags were used a great deal,

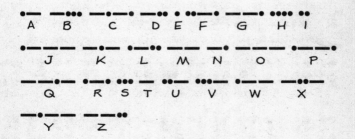

after which wireless communication quickly took over.

Wireless messages were sent using Morse Code, invented around 1837 by Samuel Morse. When he invented the code, he made sure that the letters used most frequently (E and T) were the easiest to send (· and −). Here is the full code, but of course, to make it secret, the letters would be jumbled up using a transposition code.

This system of dots and dashes can also be written another way, using a base-line as the gaps between letters or words, with a small peak for a dot and a taller peak for a dash.

When written like this, morse looks like a series of electrical impulses, and of course electrical impulses are what we use to communicate with today. Speech, music and television pictures are all transformed into chains of electrical impulses before they are passed down wires, through glass-fibre cables, then broadcast over the airwaves or beamed up to satellites, to be bounced back to some other distant spot on Earth.

As well as the many complicated communications codes, we still need and use some quite simple codes today. Blind people can read using a system of raised dots called Braille, which is read by touch, using both hands. The dots are placed within a six-spot domino pattern, and there are separate codes for music, electrical circuitry, and so on. When you think about it, this grid is very similar to the seven-bar grid used on pocket calculators to produce representations for numbers.

There is a very old and popular symbol code which uses a similar grid, called the Pig Pen code:

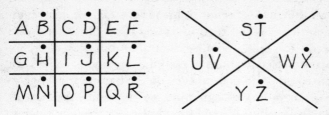

And here is another version of the Pig Pen code, which just uses the noughts and crosses grid, repeated three times. For this you need three code words, each of three letters, to make it work. Let's choose three abbreviated days of the week: Mon, Wed and Fri.

Write your code words along the top line of the grid, and then fill in the other available spaces with the rest of the alphabet. There is one space left over, and it's a good idea to fill this with the letter E, so that you have two options for that letter. Can you decode this message? As a clue, 7 usually *is* one, but 13 isn't.

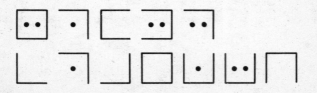

As technology improves, so there are more and more ways for us to read information. There are even machines that can read print and turn it into synthetic speech for blind people. A similar but less complex system is used in shops to read the 'bar codes' which are printed on packets (and even on the back of this book!). An electronic pen can pick up the information and decode it in a second. On this page there are what appear to be two bar codes. In fact, they are the names

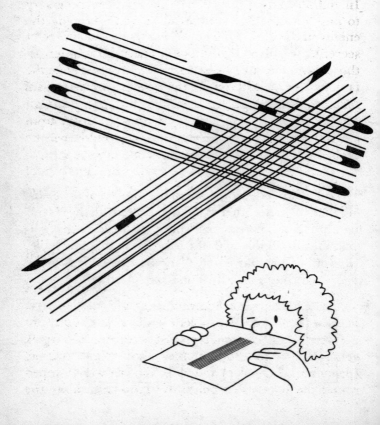

of my two sons; to read them, all you need to do is raise the book so that you are looking horizontally across the page at the 'codes'.

# Keeping Greek Secrets Secreted

In military situations, it has always been necessary to pass information to your allies, while keeping the enemy in the dark. One notable early method of secret secreting was used by the Greek general, Lisander. In those days, messages were carried by runners, like the famous hero who brought the good news twenty-six miles to Marathon . . . and then dropped dead on arrival! Now the problem with runners, apart from dropping dead on arrival, was that they could easily be ambushed and their messages be stolen. Some form of secret code or cipher was needed, some method of making Greek messages all Greek to everyone. As a result, whenever Lisander received a message, he would read it and then destroy it – he might just as well, as the message was totally meaningless. The true message was carried on the runner's belt, which looked a bit like our drawing on the next page.

There appears to be a meaningless jumble of letters on the belt; even if you know the message is hidden here, deciphering it is still a problem – especially if you're not a Greek general. You see, Lisander, like all Greek generals, carried a short staff of office called a 'scitale' (pronounced sit-a-lee) and when the belt was wrapped round the scitale in a spiral overlapping fashion, the

W A C DO E EL L LO WO BO

CD NT NX TM ME JB FT SA

COD MA TTL TI IX FX EH SI UV

UR MN LZ RA PT RE Y!

message could be clearly read. To decipher *our* message, you need to trace this belt out on to another piece of paper using a pencil, and then work out what to use

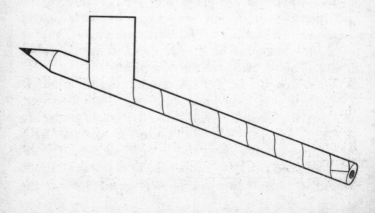

as a scitale. Perhaps you could work it out and come up with the write solution . . . Have a go.

# Caesing on a Good Idea

From Greeks to Romans. Julius Caesar, apart from having a month named after him, also gave his name to the simple sliding cipher which he is supposed to have used. Basically it works like this. First, the alphabet is written down, then it is placed below another copy of the same alphabet and slid along an agreed number of places to the left. For instance, with Caesar Cipher 7, the second alphabet is slid seven places to the left, to look like this:

ABCDEFGHIJKLMNOPQRSTUVWXYZ
ABCDEFGHIJKLMNOPQRSTUVWXYZABCDEFG

In use, BEWARE THE IDES OF MARCH

becomes: ILDHYL AOL PKLZ VM THYJO

At first glance, the code seems to hide the message well; however, for an expert code-cracker, deciphering it would be easy. The frequency with which letters occur is one of the main tools used by code-breakers. In the English language, for every 100 letters, the letter E occurs on average thirteen times (that's once every six letters). The letter T occurs about nine times, A and O about eight times, and so on. J, K, Q, X and Z occur on average less than one per cent of the time. Here is a

ABCDEFGHIJKLMNOPQRSTUVWXYZ

ABCDEFGHIJKLMNOPQRSTUVWXYZ

percentage frequency tally; above each letter, a sort of city skyline type graph has been drawn. Below it is a similar graph based on the letter frequency in our short message. Because it contained only twenty letters, we have to multiply the results by five to get rough percentages. (For instance, the letter L features four times, and so gets a tally of $4 \times 5 = 20$.) At first, the two graphs look very different, but when the second one is slid along by seven places to the left, it matches the first one remarkably well, especially the E and A towers and the troughs for J, K, X, Y and Z. With longer messages, the pattern is usually even easier to spot.

The English language has many unusual characteristics which form tools in the code-breaker's armoury. Here are just a few:

- half of all English words begin with the letters A, O, S, T or W
- half of all English words end with the letters D, E, S or T
- all English words contain at least one of the vowels A, E, I, O, U or Y

- the five most frequent two-letter words are OF, TO, IN, IT and IS
- the five most frequent three-letter words are THE, AND, FOR, ARE and BUT

With these tools at your disposal, you can ask your friends to produce a message using a Caesar or 'sliding' cipher, and they'll be amazed at just how quickly you can decipher it . . . which is why for many years now the majority of coded messages have been sent in the form of cryptograms.

# Cryp togr amme ssag eset

Cryptograms are series of letters in groups, usually of three, four or five. The title above reads 'cryptogram messages', and two letters have been added at the end to make up the last group of four letters. This might be another typical message:

WTIDH AHNOO TEKIW CTITE HHTST

The message looks completely hidden, but to decipher it you simply stack the groups on top of each other like this:

```
W T I D H
A H N O O
T E K I W
C T I T E
H H T S T
```

and, reading downwards, you get 'Watch the Think It Do It Show', with two random letters added to make up the groups.

Now you know the system, here is the same message with a very slight variation:

EHINK VTATI WEWCT OHTHD HSTIO

This time, after stacking the groups, you have to read it in a spiral starting at the centre and working outwards:

```
E H I N K
V T A T I
W E W C T
O H T H D
H S T I O
```

Another simple way of scrambling a simple message is to divide the number of letters in half and alternate the two halves:

```
W A T C H T H E T H I N
 K I T D O I T S H O W
```

Then, taking the letters in groups of three, you get:

WKA ITT CDH OTI HTE STH HOI WNE

(with a random letter tacked on the end).

To further confuse, you can add a random letter to the beginning of each group to get:

BWKA FITT OCDH BOTI ZHTE VSTH MHOI PWNQ

Now, even though you know the original message, you can see how simple yet effective this method can be. See if you can work out the pattern for this message:

BWOH ESTI MODT PIKN ZIHT
PEHT EHCT SAWN

or this one:

BWOH SVTI ODPT IKNA AIHT EIHT
HCMT AWET.

Rather than remember a system which can change from time to time, it is really better to use the same system but have a governing *code word* that changes from time to time. For our code word, let's choose the word 'numbers'. To code your message, you simply write the message under the code word:

**N U M B E R S**
4 7 3 1 2 5 6
W A T C H T H
E T H I N K I
T D O I T S H
O W P T I S B

You then number the columns according to the alphabetical order of the letters in the code word. Taking the columns of letters in numerical order, you get:

1 2 3 4 5 6 7
C H T W T H A
I N H E K I T
I T O T S H D
T I P O S B W

and when the columns become rows, they read:

CIIT HNTI THOP WETO TKSS
HIHB ATDW

which looks very scrambled indeed but which can easily be deciphered, providing you know the code word.

You can also use a code word to scramble the alphabet and then use a transposition code. This one has the added advantage that each letter is represented by another letter, but not always by the same letter every time.

First write your code word, and then list the rest of the alphabet, in a five-by-five grid (note that I and J occupy the same space to make the 26 letters fit).

N U M B E
R S A C D
F G H IJ K
L O P Q T
V W X Y Z

Then take your message and split it into pairs of letters:

WA TC HT HE TH IN KI TD OI TS HO WB

You now transpose each pair of letters according to their position in the grid. If the two letters are not in the same row or column, they will form opposite corners of a square or rectangle of letters, and you swap each letter for the letter in the opposite corner in the same row (so W A becomes X S, and T C becomes Q D). If the pair of letters should appear in the same row, swap each one for the next letter to the right. If the pair appear in the same column, swap each letter for the one below it. (So,

in our message, K I becomes F K, and T D becomes
Z K.)

The finished message looks like this:

XS QD KP KM PK FB FK ZK QG OD GP YU

Messages in this form are very difficult to decipher. The
letter K appears five times, but only the first three stand
for H. The last two represent I and D. T appears five
times represented by Q, P, P, Z and O.

# Answers

Take 'SIX LETTERS' away to leave 'NUMBERS'.

## Play on Words

'After finishing my correspondence, walked to dependable restaurant and dined on roast beef followed by an excellent rhubarb and custard.'

SURORORORORORROR – survivor (sur-five-or)
TTTTFIED – fortified (four-t-fied)
MENMENMENDOUS – tremendous (three-men-dous)
ISISISISISISISISISIS – tennis (ten-is)

## Cryptogram Messages

(B)WOH (E)STI (M)ODT (P)IKN (Z)IHT (P)E
HT (E)HCT (S)AW(N):
Remove all first letters and read backwards!

(B)WOHS(V)TIOD(P)TIKN(A) (A)IHTE(I)H
THC(M)T AW(ET):
Remove the first letter from the first group, the second

letter from the second group, the third letter from the third group, the fourth letter from the fourth group, then repeat the pattern. Read from right to left, too.

# CHAPTER 10

# Strictly for Squares

Why are boxing rings square? If they were round, you couldn't sit in the corners. This chapter revolves around squares. Square squares – not round squares – although you do need to look around for a square piece of card or paper. Any size will do, as long as you can hold it in two hands.

Now how many sides has your square piece of card got? If you haven't got a square piece of card, it won't have any, but if you do get a square piece of card, the answer to 'How many sides has it got?' is six. Oh, yes it has. It has the four sides on the four sides, and also the front side and the back side (if you'll pardon the expression). Anyway, it's these last two sides we're interested in for this 'triffic trick'. Simply mark two arrows on the card, one on the front side pointing upwards and one on the other side pointing sideways, just like the one in the picture. Hold your card by two corners as shown, and you are ready for your first performance – that's if there's anyone watching.

You see the arrow on the front is pointing upwards to the top side; but if you twist the corners in your fingers and turn the card over, you'll see that the arrow on the other side is also pointing to the top side. If you keep turning it, you'll find you have an arrow on each side pointing to the top side. Now turn the card so that the

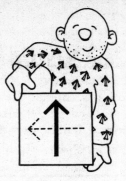

arrow on the front side is pointing to the right side. Providing you still hold the card exactly as in the diagram, when you twist the corners to turn it over you will find that the arrow on the other side is pointing to the left side. This means you have an arrow on each side pointing to opposite sides. Are you suitably baffled? Then try the trick all over again, only this time hold the card by the other two diagonal corners. This time you'll get an arrow on the front side pointing to the top side, and an arrow on the other side pointing to the bottom side. Confusing, isn't it?

# Get Out of That

This trick is not about arrows, but it does relate to one man's 'arrowing experiences. It appears that there was a convict with arrows on his uniform who was locked up in a very special prison. The prisoner was languishing in one of the twenty-five cells of the prison (see our diagram) when the jailer arrived with news that he could leave the prison, provided that on his way out he stepped into every cell once and once only. Internally, there is a door in every wall, so that all the cells are connected to one another. But the only door to the outside world is in the bottom left-hand corner – just one cell away from our convict. Can you find a route that will take him into every cell once and out through the door? You may find it difficult to do without missing one square, but it *is* possible.

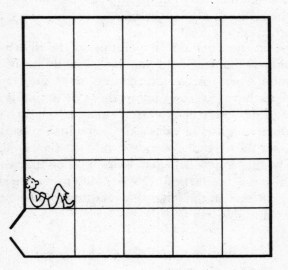

# Chess for Your Amusement

Most of the following tricks and puzzles are to do with a chess or draughts board, and it will be useful if you have one handy. However, these next few puzzles involve cutting up a chessboard – but don't do that with yours, you'll spoil it.

# Domi – No

Just imagine a chessboard like this one, with the two corner squares missing. Now imagine you have thirty-one dominoes, each just big enough to cover two squares on the board. The question is, can you lay your thirty-one dominoes on the board covering the sixty-two squares exactly?

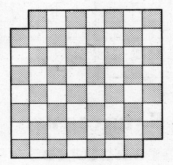

# Two More Missing Squares

For this puzzle you need to make a chessboard out of paper, and then cut it into two pieces diagonally along the line shown in Diagram A. Now everyone knows that a chessboard has sixty-four squares, but here's how you can make some of the squares disappear. Just slide the top section down along the cut line, and line up the lines once again as in our second diagram (B). Now count the squares: there are seven rows of nine squares, with two half-squares missing ($7 \times 9 = 63 - 1 = 62$). Where have the other two squares gone?

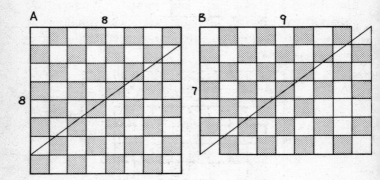

# Sliding Squares are Unsquare Squares

While you are in the drawing and cutting mood, you can make a really effective optical illusion in just a couple of minutes. You need to draw this special chess-board on paper, and then cut it carefully along the heavy line to form two pieces that slot into each other. Now you will see that slight sideways movements will produce the really strong optical illusion that the rows of squares are getting narrower at one end and wider at the other.

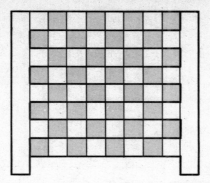

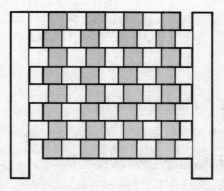

# A Far from Easy
# Jigsaw Puzzle

Before you put away your scissors, draw another chessboard and cut it into pieces along the heavy lines in our
diagram. Shuffle the pieces and close this book, then try
to reassemble the board. This really is a very difficult
jigsaw. It's even hard if, while shuffling the pieces, you

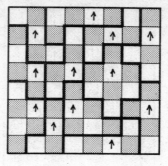

keep them the same way up as they were originally . . .
If you want to, you can even mark each piece with an
arrow pointing up, so that they don't get twisted round.
Trying to solve this should fill an hour or two.

## What a Pentomime

Dominoes are formed by joining two squares together.
But why stop at two squares? Other ominoes can be
formed by joining more squares together: three, four, or
even five. The American mathematician, Solomon W.
Golomb, wrote a book called *Polyominoes* which ex-
plored many of the omino possibilities, and he even
invented a game called 'Pentominoes' that you might
find amusing. First of all, the problem is to find all the
possible pentominoes – that is ominoes formed by
joining five squares together. The squares are not going
to be numbered, so the shapes have no particular top
side – you can turn them over if you like. So the two
shapes opposite count as one. In fact, there are twelve
possible five-square ominoes. See if you can draw them

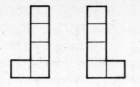

all before you check the answer at the end of the chapter. Once you've found the twelve pentominoes, you might like to make a set. If you make them with squares the same size as your chessboard squares, then you can have a go at Professor Golomb's two games.

In the first game, the first player takes any piece and places it on the chessboard so that it covers five squares. The second player then takes another piece and places that on the chessboard. The object is to be the one who places the last piece, and this is achieved when no remaining piece can fit over five uncovered squares.

An alternative to this game is first to divide the twelve pieces by choosing alternately. Lay the pieces out in front of you, so that they can be seen by both of you. Now, as you place each of your pieces, you try to make the best move, preventing your opponent from placing his remaining pieces. Good games, good games!

# Ten Ticklish Teasers

If you have gone to the trouble of making a set of pentominoes, here are ten puzzles that will keep you and your friends occupied for hours. First remove from the set of twelve pentominoes the 'cross' and the M-shaped pentominoes, as you won't be needing them. Now all you have to do is to select any one of the remaining pentominoes as your 'model'; with the other nine pentominoes, you can construct the same 'model' shape again, only three times as tall and three times as wide. I have given solutions for two of them at the end of the chapter, but I leave you to find the other eight.

## Four-way Splits

Here are two puzzles you can try, the object in each case being to divide a chessboard into four equal parts. Try these puzzles with pencil and paper. In the first puzzle, four squares have been marked 1, 2, 3 and 4. The idea is to divide up the board into four identical-shaped pieces, each containing just one of the numbers. As a clue, each of the four centre squares features in a different piece, so in our diagram I have already marked the centre dividing lines.

In the second puzzle, the object is the same, but here more numbers have been given to help you. We want four identical-shaped pieces, each containing one of each of the numbers 1, 2, 3 and 4. To start you off, I have drawn the dividing line between each pair of like numbers. As the four shapes will be identical, each dividing line will need to be repeated four times so that the pattern is the same (I have already done that for the lines which separate the figures 1), no matter which edge of the board you are viewing from. If you do the same with the rest, you'll be almost there.

# Queens in a Quandary

Chess players will know that the Queen is the most powerful piece on a chessboard, but you don't have to be able to play chess to try to solve the quandary of the eight Queens. A chess Queen has the power to move any number of squares either vertically, horizontally or diagonally, which means that the Queen can attack any piece that is in the same row or column as herself, or on the same diagonal. The problem here is to place eight Queens on the board so that no Queen is in the same row or column, or on the same diagonal line, as any of the others. (Of course you can use any old objects – say, eight pawns – to represent the eight Queens.) There is only one solution to this problem, but the solution looks different if viewed from a different side of the board, or seen through a mirror. Why not give it a try, and if you find it troublesome, then use one or more of the following three clues. The first clue is that no Queens occupy any of the squares on the two long diagonals. If you start by placing the first Queen in the first column on the lowest square possible, then clue number two is that the Queen in column two is on the same colour square.

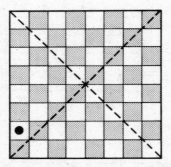

With the third clue, the problem becomes so easy as to solve itself – so try the problem without it first. (If you do need it, the third clue is that the Queen in the fourth column is also on the same colour square.)

# Roll Over and Die

In the shops a few years ago, there was a game played on a chessboard with rolling dice as pieces. (Dice is plural, and *one* of them is called a 'die', which partly explains the title, above.) Each die fitted neatly on to a square, and you made a move by rolling the die over on its edge – either in straight or in zigzag lines, according to the number showing on the top of the die at the start of the move. So a die with a single dot on top could roll just once to the next square, either forward or backward or to the left or the right. After the move, a new number would be showing on top, giving the piece a new value for its next move. As well as the number on the top of the die, the numbers on the sides of the die are important: they help to determine which number will be on top at the end of the move. By zigzagging, there is usually more than one way to arrive at a particular square, and different routes result in different numbers ending up on top. The diagrams show the possible moves of a die with a two on top and with a three on top – and you can imagine that moves for four, five and six get more complicated.

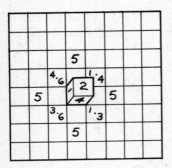

However, here are two much simpler but very interesting tasks. Place a die in the top left-hand corner of your chessboard and note its top number . . . let's say it is 6. Can you roll the die from square to square, visiting each square on the board once and once only, but never allowing the 6 to appear on the top until it reaches the final square in the top right-hand corner? You can start by rolling to the right for three squares, but then you have to change direction because the fourth roll would bring the 6 to the top again. So roll down one square. If you roll left for three squares, the 6 will be on top again, but you can get to that second square down on the left without the 6 appearing on top – by zigzagging. Go left, down, left, up, then left, and you find the 6 is now on the right-hand side of the die; this means that you can roll the die all the way down the side of the board to the bottom left-hand corner. Now you have already covered sixteen squares. Use a pencil and paper to record your moves and see if you can complete the tour of the board. At the end, the pattern is symmetrical, with the right-hand side of the board a mirror image of the left-hand side. Have a go. If you get stuck, the answer is at the end of the chapter, but if you do look at the answer, look for a brief second only and then see if you can find the way round by yourself.

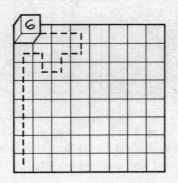

If you enjoyed that puzzle, here is another one. Place the die in the top left-hand corner, but this time with the 6 on the side of the die that faces you and the bottom edge of the board. From there it is possible to tour the board and arrive back where you started without the 6 ever showing on top of the die. Once again, discounting mirror images, there is only one solution – and this solution is symmetrical from top to bottom instead of from left to right. Have a try, and good touring.

# A Moving Trick

Here is a trick we used on one of the 'Think of a Number' shows. The trick is performed on a draughts board, which is the same as a chessboard, only turned on its side, so that there is a white square in the bottom left-hand corner. Next to that white square there is a row of three white squares in a diagonal line, and there's an identical line of three white squares in the opposite top right-hand corner.

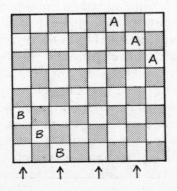

Before performing the trick with a friend, you need to demonstrate what you want them to do. Place three draughtsmen or chessmen on one of the rows of three white squares A-A-A or B-B-B. Explain that while your back is turned, they are to choose whether to start from A-A-A or from B-B-B. All they have to do then is to move the three counters one diagonal square at a time, just like kings in the game of draughts (that means they can move in any direction diagonally, including backwards, only staying on the white squares). They can move the counters in any order, any number of moves, but for each move they must count aloud. Ask them to stop after they have made an even number of moves, somewhere between 10 and 20. Remind them that they can choose which three squares they start on while your back is turned; and say that when they have made the moves, you will tell them which three squares they started from. When they have made their moves and you turn round again, one look at the board is all you need to work out where they started from.

Here is how you do it. Simply count the number of counters in the four columns arrowed in the diagram (the ones with a white square on the bottom row). If the total is one or three (odd numbers) then they must have started with an odd number in those columns, which means they must have started in the top right-hand corner. If the number is nought or two (even numbers), they must have started in the bottom left-hand corner. To make the trick more mystifying, you can allow them to leapfrog one piece over another, as in draughts, without including the jumps in the number of moves (for example, 'One, two, three, jump, four, jump, five, etc.'). This works because a jump moves a counter two columns, and so doesn't alter the odd or even count.

One last thing: if you wanted to move the three counters from one set of starting squares to the other, it would take 15 normal moves. But if I were to allow you to make jumps – without counting them – what would be the smallest number of moves needed to get your three counters to the opposite corner? Remember, you count the moves, but you don't count the jumps.

## The Final Frame

Finally, here is a phenomenon strictly for squares that is really magic and diabolically clever. In *Think Box*, I featured a chapter on magic squares, but here is a magic square that magically changes its shape from a square into a three-dimensional frame. Let's start with a diabolic magic square in which each row and each column adds up to 34.

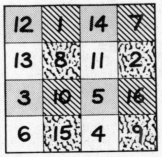

A

But notice that any group of four numbers in a square also adds up to 34. Clever, isn't it? Now if you were to cut that square out, you could fold it to form a four-sided tube, like this.

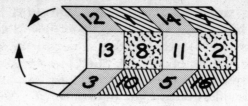

B

Now imagine this square tube was made of stretchy rubber and you could bend and stretch it so that the two open ends met, but it still kept its square shape. Then it would look rather like this and you would have a Diabolic Magic Frame.

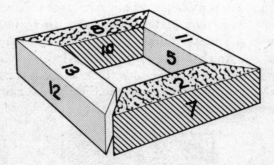

C

Would you like one? Well, here's one that you can trace or copy on to stiffer paper, then cut, fold and glue it to form your very own Diabolic Magic Frame.

What is so magic about it, now that you have made it? Well, each of its four faces – top, bottom, inside and outside – is made up of a group of four numbers that add up to 34. Not only that, our diagram shows the numbers shaded in four different ways: each group of numbers shaded in the same way also adds up to 34. And what's more, the frame has sixteen corners with four faces meeting at each corner; every one of those

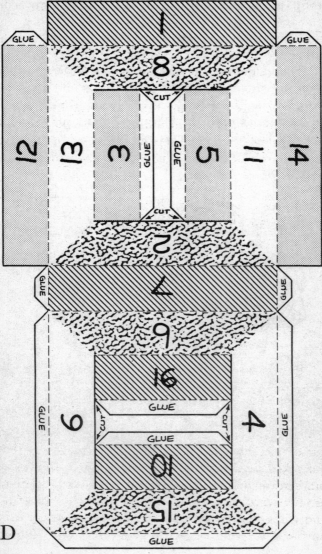

groups of four faces adds up to 34. The four numbers on each arm of the frame also add up to 34, and when you view the frame from one corner (as in diagram C) you will notice that the four faces facing you (12, 7, 10 and 5) also add up to 34 – and there are four corners to view from, so four similar groups of faces that add up to 34. Keep looking, because if you take a spiral path round the frame once again, each group of four numbers adds up to 34. Diabolically clever, isn't it?

# Answers

## Get Out of That

Remember the instructions were that the prisoner must step into *every* cell once and once only. That must include his own cell, so what he does is to step into the next cell and then back into his own cell, and then it is quite easy to find a route which visits every remaining cell on the way out.

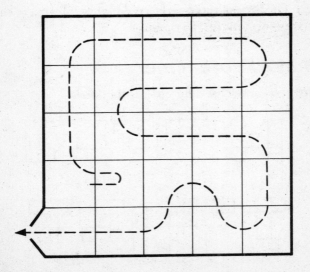

# Domi – No

The answer to the domino puzzle is 'NO'. Although there are 62 squares and 31 double-square dominoes, you can't make the dominoes fit over the squares. If you look at the diagram again, you will see that the two missing squares are both 'white'. Each domino can only cover one black and one white square; so, no matter how you place the dominoes, you will end up with one domino and two black squares left over.

## Two More Missing Squares

If you make this puzzle and try it, you will find that to line up the two halves, as shown in our diagram (p. 156), one piece has to overlap the other along the diagonal edge. The area of this overlap is equal to the area of the two missing squares, so there.

## What a Pentomime

Here are the twelve different pentominoes:

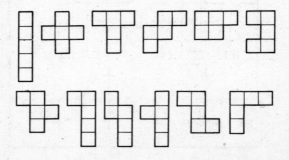

# *Ten Ticklish Teasers*

Just two of the ten solutions:

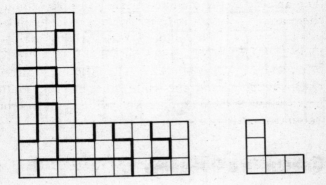

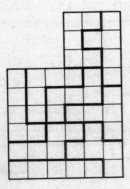

# *Four-way Splits*

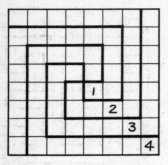

# **Queens in a Quandary**

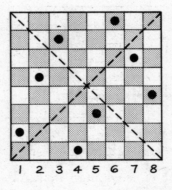

# Roll Over and Die

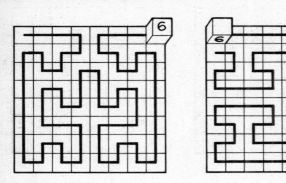

# A Moving Trick

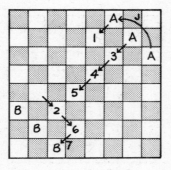

You can move three counters from A-A-A to B-B-B – not counting jumps – in just 7 moves. Make move 1 and then with 5 consecutive jumping moves you can get one piece home. Then make sideways move 2 and move the centre piece, 3, 4 and 5, and then jump it home, leaving two more moves (6 and 7) for the last piece.